Dead relatives will roll over in their graves,
so don't let them know you're reading
   THE UNAMUSEMENT PARK.
Stranger things have rarely happened
in your own night terrors or on
episodes of *THE TWILIGHT ZONE.*
Follow Jacob, a mattress delivery driver,
who loses himself in an infinite hallway
of colored doors. Each door is the threshold
to a new altered reality. Sublime dreams
mix with surreal nightmares. Is this
Aldous Huxley's famous *DOORS OF
PERCEPTIONS,* of some cruel virtual
reality experiment? Some people, like
Jacob, might look for an escape from this
House of Mindgames, but others will look at
our modern lives as the real nightmare. How
about you? Would you look for escape or make
               yourself at home in
         THE UNAMUESMENT PARK?

THE UNAMUSEMENT PARK

a novel

by Walter Black

The Unamusement Park

© 2005 by Walter Black

Library of Congress

Fiction: altered realities,
dreams, fantasies

cover artwork by the author
backpage photo: Lulu gallery
author photo last page:
Jon Delacruz

ISBN: 978-0-6152-4338-2

Library of Congress
Control Number 2008907944

"To make biological survival possible, Mind at Large has to be funneled through the reducing valve of the brain and nervous system. What comes out at the other end is a measly trickle of the kind of consciousness which will help us to stay alive on the surface of this particular planet......That which, in the language of religion, is called "this world" is the universe of reduced awareness, expressed, and, as it were, petrified by language. The various "other worlds' which human beings erratically make contact are so many elements in the totality of the awareness belonging to Mind at Large. Most people, most of the time, know only what comes through the reducing valve and is consecrated as genuinely real by the local language. Certain persons, however, seem to be born with a kind of by-pass that circumvents the reducing valve. In others, temporary by-passes may be acquired either spontaneously, or as the result of deliberate "spiritual exercises," or through hypnosis, or by means of drugs."

ALDOUS HUXLEY
from The Doors of Perception (1954)

"If the doors of perception were cleansed every thing
would appear to man as it is, infinite."

WILLIAM BLAKE

"...All writing of the narrative kind, and perhaps all writing, is
motivated, deep down, by a fear of and a fascination with
mortality – by a desire to make the risky trip to the Underworld,
and to bring back something or someone back from the dead.
You may find the subject a little peculiar. It is a little peculiar.
Writing itself is a little peculiar."

MARGARET ATWOOD
from Negotiating with the Dead (2002)

THE UNAMUSEMENT PARK

"You shouldn't have come here. I would advise you to retrace your steps. Read these words backwards, from right to left. Make a hasty retreat. Close this book and erase the title from your memory banks. Completely and absolutely "un-discover" this text. No, I guess not. This is all wishful thinking on my part. I am oh-so-sorry, it's too late. You're in. Apparently, you are the Pandora's-Box type. No insult intended here, but if you were to misplace this booklet among the others, believe me, you'd be doing yourself a great service. Unfortunately, there will remain that miniscule itch, that insistent little voice in the backside of your consciousness. The voice will innocently ask you, "What was that all about?" The question yearns to be answered, as surely as an itch must be scratched. The riddle will beg to be solved."

"Well then, since I observe that you've continued, you may as well make yourself cozy. Pull up a chair, as they say (whoever they are). I'd so love to tell you everything. You look intelligent, quizzical, a real go-getter. How would I possibly tell you everything? - - - - - - - Oh, that old biddy up there? She's our very own Laughing Lady. What a shame we cannot hear from her anymore, poor old gal. Her power chord must have shorted-out long ago. Spooky, how she stands so motionless, arms spread, with her portentous, Cheshire-cat smile and that puffy face of hers, all caked in makeup and rouge. At times I could swear that I hear her cackling. Her laughter seems to drift in from far away, as if echoing from a canyon. It's the sound of a memory from an ancient ghost story."

"Oh dear, but as for you, my friend. Please forgive me, I sincerely wish I could show you the way out. I used to assume, long ago, that there was a back door to this place. My assumption was the inept conclusion of a simpleton. I arrived here exactly that – a simpleton. My thoughts ran a rigid and limited course that I liked to call logic. If every place I 'd ever entered by the front door had also a back door – then, surely, this place with its front door would logically have a back door, also. Or so I thought. Well, let me tell you, logic has long since gone the way of the dodo. Along with a back door, logic is not to be found here. I have looked, and searched. I have prayed and even visualized it. A back door refuses to present itself. We find ourselves (you and me), in a residence with an entrance, but lacking entirely any manner of exit. I know, I know. It's not possible, you will say. I used to say that myself. If only I had told you right off, "Sorry, you must have the wrong address." I could have rudely slammed the door in your face, sending you on your merry way. I presume your way was merry?"

"Here, then, here we are. Obviously, you've made it past the front door, the first door. Allow me to usher you in through the second door. There you are, and there you have it. We keep the keys up here on this brass ring hanging from a hook. The keys are all, each and every one of them, old skeleton keys. Here, you take the whole ring of them. Old keys are said to open old locks. That may sound innocent enough, but behind the doors…but, well, hmm, let me say no more, lest I bore you with mere words. You are free to try out the keys for yourself. From this point on, quite frankly, I would only be in your way. Therefore, I'll now bid you a fond ado. I must add that I wish you the very best. You will be on your own now. It was a pleasure, I do say, with all due respect."

He opens the first door to the left of the long hallway, enters briefly, leaving the door ajar. He reappears and steps partially into the hallway to hang a sign on the door that reads DO NOT DISTURB. As he turns his back on me, he then twitters his fingers over his shoulder, his quaint manner of waving goodbye. He re-enters the room, now marked DO NOT DISTURB, and gently pulls the door shut. I hear the door latch and then I hear the dead-bolt lock.

It crosses my mind, only at this instant, that I have said not one word of reply to his introduction. I didn't even ask the eccentric little guy for his name. The hallway, where he left me standing, is disturbingly long. I stand, dumbfounded, with a large ring of keys in my hand, staring at a teetering DO NOT DISTURB sign. I face the overwhelming row of doors and light fixtures, growing smaller and smaller into the distant corridor. In reaction to this I turn around. Who cares if there is no back door? I'll exit by way of the front door. Upon turning, I am startled to encounter a person behind me, also turning to notice me. My breath freezes in my chest and my heart stops. In the dim light, I then recognize that the other person is me. It is my reflection in a full-length mirror on the backside of the door. The dark reflection is unnerving. The infinite hallway is now doubled in length by the mirror. With an exhale of relief, I notice a crystal doorknob and reach for it, anxious to retreat out the front door. Unexpectedly, however, the doorknob gives way to my grasp as if hung on a string. My hand, holding the floating doorknob, lunges forward into the reflection. Within the mirror my hand becomes invisible. I pull back abruptly. I have seen these mirrors in movies, usually black-and-white movies. The mirrors in motion pictures always radiate rings of watery ripples, but this mirror is like air, and I am minus one hand until I yank it back out.

I'm not really up for a full-body disappearing act, so I do another about-face. Such an incredibly long hallway! The two walls and the endless doors seem to merge where the ceiling and floor converge on the far off horizon. From the looks of it, the hallway stretches beyond the horizon. My attempt at retreat was thwarted by the trick mirror, but I'm not really up for a long walk either. I take a few cautious steps forward. I wish I had worn sneakers today. These dress shoes make a clunking noise on the hardwood floor. I walk, instead, on tiptoe. The ring of keys jingles no matter how I walk. So many keys, and so many doors. I'm not used to unlocking a strange door that doesn't enter my own room. I'm a firm believer in respecting the privacy of others.

Speaking of others, the odd little guy, who ushered me in, didn't mention others. Or did he? Not that I recall, anyway. I'll try knocking on one of the doors. What if someone is sleeping inside? I hate disturbing anyone's sleep.

I resume tiptoeing down the hallway past several doors. Each door is painted its own color: yellow, blue, green, orange, gray, black, purple, red, salmon, magenta, aqua, pink. I refuse to knock on a pink door. I'm drawn to the blue door, but it seems to suggest that someone is sleeping. For gosh sakes, I may as well pick a door and knock. Green. That's a neutral color. It even means go. I raise my knuckles to knock on the door. "Go on, knock." (I have to talk myself into it.) Knock, knock, knock. The sound is so empty. I wait for a reply. I wait a little longer. Knock, knock, knock. Why am I knocking only three times? Knock, knock, knock, knock, knock. Nothing, still no answer.

I've been warned that this disconcerting dwelling has no exit and that logic is not to be found here. Obviously, it's a trick. I'm the victim of a prankster. Some sadistic joker has set me up. Whoever this mysterious, demented demon is, he or she has instructed the nerdy little doorman to hand me these God-awful keys. Some sick, twisted, conniving jerk expects me to fall for this obvious trap. "Old keys open old locks," the strange little doorman said. He did not bluntly suggest that I try the keys in the locks. I am "free to try the keys," I was told. I will, however, be left holding the blame. Inserting a key into a door's lock will be *breaking and entering*. "No, officer," I can hear my self pleading, "These are not my keys and this room was not rented, leased, nor was it sold to me." I can hear the gavel slamming upon the judge's desk, "Guilty, as charged."

I back away from the green door and shamble in self humiliation past three more doors: lavender, chartreuse, and gold. I look back down the dimly lit hallway to see my discouraged reflection in the trick-mirror. I have shrunk to the size of a toothbrush. This hallway is a macabre prison. The prospects of this hallway feel more intimidating than a claustrophobic closet.

I grunt at myself in disgust. I am falling for the demon's plan. I look at the gold door. Far too showy, to my thinking. I backtrack to the aqua door. Such a harmless and lighthearted color, aqua. Calming to the nerves. O.K., I give in. I knock three times. Three knocks seem so polite and unobtrusive; respectful. Once again there is no response. Three knocks, I wait again, and then five knocks – louder and more urgent, fast pace knocks. Once again, not a peep.

I growl at myself for being such a spineless jellyfish. I now select a key and, apparently, my better judgment has left town, gone on vacation. My fingers are inserting a key in the lock. I jiggle and readjust, then jiggle the key some more. Wrong key. Next key on the ring: I jiggle it, realign, and jiggle it some more. No, not this one either. "**What am I doing here**?" my thoughts are screaming inside my mind. The third key has specks of aqua paint that match the door perfectly. Out of desperation, my spirit lifts. I insert the aqua-specked key, and voila - the lock turns and I open the aqua door. My heart now crams itself up near my Adam's apple. I have forgotten how to breathe!

BEHIND THE AQUA DOOR

I push gently on the door, only about an inch. I don't want to bang the door against a chain lock or knock down a delicate old lady. An elderly person might be frightened to answer. The door swings wide open as if pulled by a bungee chord. I see through the doorway a scene I had not expected. I expected perhaps antique furniture, quilts, doilies and porcelain vases holding plastic roses, perhaps a spinster knitting in her rocking chair. Al contraire, the door has opened upon an outdoor playground under a dull silver sky. A tall fence boxes a yard of fine, dusty dirt. Monkey bars and a brick building stand in the background. Near me, through the Cyclone fence, a little girl, maybe seven years old, is arranging a pattern in the beige dust. She has arranged a long, wavy line of collected rock, twigs, leaves, two flattened cans, and one flattened paper cup. Her brown hair is pulled to the sides of her head by silver clips that are badly chipped, showing white plastic edges. Strands of hair have escaped the clips and fall over her face. She repeatedly tucks the loose hair behind her ears. She's wearing a black leotard top, a green pleated skirt, and black canvas shoes. She is delicately thin, but her face is noble. She has designed an anaconda in the dirt, and accentuated a center point of each curve with a small stone. I count twelve stones in twelve curves. She hums a haunting little tune, hops on one leg, and then vacillates from one foot to two feet, careful to not step on her creation. After hopping the length of the snake, she turns (teetering with arms spread for balance) and hops back, one leg, two legs, one leg, …two. She has conjured her very own version of hop scotch.

I don't recall entering this scene, but I am no longer standing in the hallway. I am now on the playground, inside the fence, watching her play. I expect her to look up. I would say hello or at least smile at her. She doesn't notice that I exist. Beyond her, I notice a white and purple soccer ball a few yards away, near the jungle gym. I walk closer to the soccer ball and discover that it is a large turnip. "Odd thing to find on a playground," I think. With my right hand, I pick it up. In my left hand I carry a stack of books piled upon a notebook, resting against my hip. I am a boy now, not a man. I enter the brick-house school, and I know my way to the cafeteria. Immersed in a crowd of students, we line up among the tables folded against the wall. My line of students is fourth graders. After the blast of the bell, we trail up the stairwell, which is old, cream-colored marble, with black veins and milk-chocolate swirls. Each step up is massive. My legs are forced to make exaggerated steps. The line of fourth-graders feeds into our classroom. Shedding our coats and gloves in the coat room is a monumental task.

The school day slips by. Was I daydreaming and forgot to pay attention? How did the final rude-sounding bell sneak up on me? I'm leaving school, my books in one hand and the turnip in the other. I don't recall pulling my coat and gloves back on. As I cross the playground I think, "This is where I found the big turnip." I step over the very spot, and the turnip slips from my hand. I turn around and there it is on the ground behind me. The turnip has a mind of its own. By repositioning itself exactly as if I had never found it, the turnip taunts me. Eerie rushes of thoughts flash through my mind: "Everything ends up where it begins. We all move about, shuffled like a deck of cards. The cards will all return to their original order. Each of us are destined to end up back at the beginning. The turnip's roundtrip journey was a glaring clue, screaming to me that everything cancels itself out. I've stumbled upon nihilism. The world, my mind, my body, and my life are all delusion, a mere card trick. I don't really exist, the world does not exist." These wordy thoughts rush to me in the time span of a gasp, a mere snap recognition. Meteors and blurred stars hurl past me. The universe caves in. I've become a vacuum hurling through streaking comets in cold, coal-black outer space. A terrifying thrill, I am the fastest boy in all existence, burning up in a fireball of disintegration. I cease to exist. I am exhilarated and alarmed. I panic. The duration of mere seconds of this panic is excruciating.

Here I am in the hallway again. My heart is convulsing to break out of its ribcage. Where is the aqua door? I've lost track of the little girl on the playground and the overtly surreal turnip. I lie here, exhausted and curled up on the wood floor of the endless hallway. Tiny as a mouse hole on the horizon, a splinter of light reflects off the mirror on the door at the entrance of the corridor. The mirror is a tiny sequin. I find my arms and legs like a newborn colt. Miraculously, I stand, legs trembling. Turning away from the far off mirror, I walk. My dress shoes are horseshoes; clomp, clomp, clomping on the hardwood floors. I opt for tiptoeing. Up ahead, a light emanates from the floor. Approaching the light, I make out a glass or Plexiglas floor. Hesitantly, I walk out onto the glass floor. There are bubbles below me, and aquarium beneath my feet. I am delighted and baffled as scores of rabbits swim in the water under glass. I have never thought of rabbits swimming, but there they are; a school of rabbits, ears pulled back, front paws extended forward, and back legs that push back strong little frog kicks. Kicking simultaneously, they surge forward, reminding me of the breath-like motion of jellyfish. Is this some sort of Alice in Wonderland joke? This joke I can handle. I prefer swimming rabbits any day to losing my body at warp speed.

VIRTUAL REALITY

The rabbits move on and I see beneath me the undulation of long tendons of seaweed. The swaying is soothing. I feel hypnotized. An image crosses my mind of myself leaning back in a dentist chair, shot up with Novocain, and high on laughing gas. The dentist has braced my arms with straps and metal restraints and a computer helmet encases my head. He is a subversive, posing as a dentist, and he is testing his virtual reality equipment on me. I have become a guinea pig for his laboratory experiment.

What is this virtual reality, anyway? The dentist / subversive is recording my subconscious thoughts and my deep-sleep dreams. He seems to be replaying these subterranean visions for the viewing of my conscious mind. For all I know, this mad scientist is feeding me the dreams and hidden thoughts of other people. Perhaps he is collecting data for his master thesis about the collective subconscious. As he is on the verge of becoming a billionaire, I am merely one of his unsuspecting (so he thinks) lab rats.

I don't remember signing up for this. I demand my percent of his profits. And furthermore, what if I experience horrifying side effects or permanent brain damage? How much money will it take to fix my brain? What use will money be to me if I'm left mentally ill? Needless to say, I am not a happy camper. If it's the last thing I do, I will get this guy. I'm going to turn him over to the authorities. When I am aroused to consciousness, I will memorize every detail of his evil, conniving face. The police sketch will be flawless. After leaving the dentist office, I'll purchase a disposable camera from the nearest pharmacy. Upon return to the pseudo-dentist's office, I will snap photos of the receptionist, the front of the building, and the address and name plate on the building's directory. If later I become disoriented or mentally affected, I'll have all the necessary evidence on my roll of film.

I know what you're thinking. You speculate that I have become overly paranoid. Well, let me tell you, buddy, if you were in this situation, you would be paranoid. Please do not jump to hasty conclusions. I can assure you I have not reached the psychotic state of paranoia. What I am experiencing is a passing thought, a very disturbing passing thought.

This virtual reality stuff is heavy duty. I am at this moment kneeling down on the floor and the wood feels convincingly real. And when I dropped that big turnip and shot through space at warp speed, my face felt like it was coming off. My hair really got messed up. This is, truth be known, an inaccurate description, considering that I had been reduced to a vacuous vapor and had no face or hair until I reappeared in this God-forsaken hallway.

I have to admit, though, that the swimming rabbits under the glass floor might be a big hit at the Metropolitan Museum of Modern Art.

Come to think of it, the absence of a back door fits quite nicely into this "virtual reality" theory of mine. If my theory is correct, I may as well go for the whole ride while I'm here. I've always wondered about virtual reality. If I get entirely fed up with the colored doors, then, hey, what the heck, I may get up the nerve to step through that frightful mirror. It's not real anyway, right? I'll just think of it as myself stepping into a computer game. When I get released from here, I'll always regret passing up the opportunity to step through that treacherous mirror.

THE YELLOW DOOR

My perspective has shifted and my spirit lifts. Thinking of this hallway of endless doors as a trap or a trick has only served to upset me. I will think of this, now, as a game, a little recreational free time. I'm on an unusual vacation in an exotic place. I tell myself this place is exotic and esoteric, the vacation of my wildest dreams. I clomp a few steps down the hallway, and then pick up the pace to a click, click, click. The keys are jingling on my hip, attached to my belt loop. A brown door, a forest green door, a powder blue door, and a yellow door are my latest choices. I choose yellow - upbeat, cheerful and vibrant. I know better, now, than to anticipate the door opening into a typical room, so I prepare myself for the unexpected. There is a brief inner struggle between my knotted stomach and the new mind set of fearless adventure, but without pause I go directly into action with the courteous knock, knock, knocking. As before, there is no response, so I expedite my knocking, five louder knocks. I count to three and still no response, so I pick out a skeleton key and insert it in the lock. It's the wrong key. "Do any of these keys have yellow paint on them?" I wonder. I don't see a key with even the remains of yellow paint, but one key does have a powder blue dot on it. Powder blue is the neighboring door, so I try out the following key on the ring. BINGO! The key turns in the lock and the door pops open slightly. Through the slender opening I see a waist-high cabinet with a Formica counter-top and square mirrors along the wall. I open the door onto a sterile room. The wall opposite the yellow door is entirely glass, with a view of tree tops and the neighboring business complex. Is this my ticket out of here? "Hello?" I call out. Again, there is no response. I step into the room and there, in the center of the room, is something that causes me to gasp and freeze up in terror. It's the dentist's chair, and exactly as I had imagined, there are metal arm braces and straps on the arms of the reclining chair. Suspended from a jointed, adjustable metal arm, there is a complicated helmet-shaped computer apparatus, resting mid-air, alongside the dentist's chair. I forget to breathe, and the frozen dread in my chest seems to outweigh my latest conviction to go for the ride and enjoy the experience. "This is just a game," I try reminding myself, and I take in a few deep breaths. I wriggle my hands, and shake my arms to loosen up the sudden tension around my neck. I breathe out with an exaggerated whoosh. I place my hand over my sternum and feel the racing heartbeat. I need to talk myself down, "This is not an electric chair. It is not even a torture device. I am looking at a virtual reality setup. This experience could be very soothing, calming, and even blissful. This is just a game, meant for enjoyment. Nobody has any reason to intentionally seek revenge or to harm me. Don't panic. Relax. Get a grip, calm down and enjoy the possibilities. This is an opportunity, not a disaster."

I know enough about fear to know that it has kept me from doing many things that I have later learned to enjoy. I take another deep breath and walk over to the dentist's chair. Isn't there anybody here to instruct me or monitor my experience? I don't even know how to turn this contraption on. Just as this occurs to me, I spot a little switch where my right hand would rest on the armrest. There are two words engraved on the metal disc beside the switch – ACTIVATE and SHUT DOWN.

My imagination pictures me riding on a magic carpet that takes a wrong turn into the mouth of a Tyrannosaurus Rex. Would I be able to remember that my right hand is resting beside the SHUT DOWN switch as the Tyrannosaurus is splintering my eardrums with his excruciating roar? Would my mind "shut down" instead, and years later I would be found a human vegetable, unable to explain to the nurses and doctors in the hospital that I was trapped in the stomach of a dinosaur? O.K. You are right. I am getting a little paranoid. "Enough of the doom impending thoughts," I tell myself. I sit down and prepare myself to go for the joyride.

I sit down, lean back, and on the ceiling is a painting of a hammock tied between palm trees on the beach with a brilliant sunset over the water. The painting helps to put me in a trusting and innocent mood. I pull down the arm brace over my left arm and tighten the straps to a comfortable firmness. The right arm has push-button settings by the thumb for lowering the arm brace and tightening the straps. When I release the button, the strap stops tightening. If I touch it again it starts loosening. I feel confident about the push button, when it occurs to me that I have no free hand for pulling the computer helmet over my head. I reach for the thumb button to loosen the right strap when the helmet lowers itself over my head. Side flaps close in over my eyes, and the helmet tightens lightly. Padded surfaces touch my cheekbones and wrap around my head like a bicycle helmet. The flaps over my eyes are like dark sunglasses, the lenses don't touch my eyes. In the darkness of the helmet I shut my eyes. I reach with my fingers to pull the switch toward the word ACTIVATE.

I'm still feeling anxiety about this, so I leave my eyes shut. The switch has been activated. I feel cool water on my toes rising slowly up to my ankles. The surface of the cool water is tickling the hair on my legs, so I open my eyes to see what's going on. I'm hovering above an expanse of ocean, with gently lapping waves up to my knees. I look down and I'm wearing a dark blue swimsuit. The swimsuit is the roaring twenties style, a one piece tank-top attached like long underwear to the trunks. The floating-in-air sensation is enjoyable and the water is calm and comfortable, not too cold. I know how to swim, so I feel no need for alarm. I am gently lowered into the water, now up to my shoulders. I begin swimming the breast stroke. The water is murky green, but it doesn't irritate my eyes. I push myself forward with frog kicks and by fanning my arms downward. My face surfaces with each stroke and I take in new air, every other stroke. A biplane flies over me, high in the sky, and I wave one arm, but the biplane continues in a straight line and leaves a trail of billowing white smoke. Ahead of me I see a glimmering light, maybe a reflection emanating from chrome or glass. I swim a little closer and I see a colossal array of floating ice. This ice is not white like an iceberg, but as clear as an ice cube in a water glass. As I swim closer I realize the ice is immense. It is a castle of ice, literally shaped with towers and spires, a rampart, an arched doorway, and arched windows. It seems to bob gently, but I realize that I'm the one bobbing, and the castle is stable in the gently splashing green sea. The sky is pouring down bright silver sunrays, and I feel a slight chill in the water as surely the castle must be melting. As much as I feel awed by the sight of the ice castle, I feel a hypnotic soothing sensation that coincides with the melting of the castle. I swim a circle around the chilly monument, and notice that the spectacle is shrinking. Now it is merely a glassy house, melting quickly into the lulling waves.

I float on my back, and a blissful carefree sentiment engulfs me and infuses me with a sense of calm and fulfillment. What a great moment, having forgotten all concerns and complications. I simply exist and that suffices. There is nothing to desire. Ahhh... Is this the middle road called nirvana? I alternate between closing my eyes as I gently drift, and opening my eyes to watch the cumulus clouds in a robin-egg blue sky.

I close my eyes again and wobble in the waves like a baby in a cradle. When I open my eyes, a shadow engulfs me. Something massive and ominous is descending upon me, a sea monster or a black octopus. I gasp for air and duck swiftly under the waves. Swimming under water feels safer, if I presume that the monster is a giant bird or winged creature. I have no choice but to surface for air, and take a quick glance over my shoulder. The sea monster is worse than I had thought. Neither an octopus, nor a large bird, the monster is a huge black hand. The darting realization that this is a game, and I am strapped to a dentist's chair gives me a jolt of courage. I turn around to face the black giant. There is, however, no man attached to the hand. In fact, it is not even a hand, but rather a gargantuan glove. I am being attacked by a glove. This glove looks like a bicycler's glove, a black synthetic weave with a Velcro strap. The glove has fingers, each one larger than my entire body. The glove is animated, as if it were a hand, and my courage leaves me as the glove lowers itself over me. I submerge and swim under water again, but as I resurface, the glove picks me up by pinching the back of the tank-top of my swimming suit. I'm amazed that my outfit doesn't rip apart. I'm being lifted, as if by a crane, to nearly two hundred feet above the water. If the glove releases me, I will surely go into shock at the moment of my body slamming the water surface far below. (Appearing in my mind are the two words SHUT DOWN, but I am unable to place any correlation between my dilemma and the two words.)

I see a sailboat tilting in the water like a tiny far away toy. The sailboat increases in size as the flying glove lowers me in the boat's direction. As I near the sailboat, I see a small girl waving her arms. She sees me. It's the little girl from the playground who played her self-created game of hopscotch. The glove lowers me onto the stern of the sailboat, and then releases me. I lie there in a puddle on the deck. The little girl disappears into the cabin. I yell out, "Wait!" and she returns with a big white towel draped over her arm. She looks me square in the face with a sad expression as she hands me the towel. "Thank you," I say as I wrap the towel around me. I turn to witness the black glove ascend into a cloud like a chess player having finished his turn. The thin girl kneels down beside me, "What happened to you?"

It's the first time I've heard her voice and it is a soft, light, feathery utterance. I watch her dark brown hair. A whimsical breeze scatters loose strands around her face.

"I'm not sure, but I think I am trapped in a game, or a trick."

"No, no, this is only my father's boat," she says with a wry grin.

She is so easy to befriend, but the thought crosses my mind that she might be part of the game. Maybe she's the enemy, disguised as my rescuer. If the glove moved me here like a chess move, maybe she is one of the opponent's pieces. In the directness of her gaze, however, I feel that I can trust her.

The girl is dressed in a nautical hat and an old fashioned dress of ecru with navy trim. She stands up and I see that she is barefoot. Such slender legs and arms, I would guess that she is malnourished, except for her composure and gracefulness. Some children are naturally wiry. Her sinewy face accentuates her large eyes and lips. She places a delicate hand into her skirt pocket, and pulls out a hidden object. She reaches out her fisted hand toward my chest. I lay out my hand face up, half expecting her to drop a black widow into my hand. She uncurls her long fingers with exaggerated languor, and then abruptly pulls back her hand to reveal a large glass marble, the size of a golf ball, in my palm. The marble is translucent, with pearlescent swirling smoke within.

"Beautiful marble," I exclaim, and before I attempt to return it to her, she turns and walks lightly back to the cabin, disappearing within. I interpret her movements to signify that the marble is a gift. I hold the small globe up to the sunlight to peer again at the pink and blue-silver swirls. As I roll the marble between my thumb and forefinger, I witness the splintering of sunrays in the smoky swirl. Within the swirl manifests an apparition that startles me – the little girl's face inside the marble. The swirls of pink and blue-silver smoke form the loose strands of her hair, and her tiny gaze pierces my own eyes. I feel as though my thoughts are being read, and I feel embarrassed at the thought of a little girl knowing my every secret. It is, however, her direct gaze that makes me feel protected, as if by an overseer.

In the confusion and surprise of the apparition, I recall the two words SHUT DOWN. This time the message sends an image to my brain, an image of me reclining in a dentist chair. A reflex occurs, triggering my fingers to flick the switch beside my right hand. There is a quick rush of cool air on my face, and a deflating, sinking feeling in my gut. I open my eyes. What a relief! I've made it back to the dentist chair. I push the thumb button that loosens the right arm straps. The right arm-brace rises simultaneously as the automatic eye lenses unfold. The computer helmet lifts above my head and I reach to loosen the straps on my left arm. The left arm brace unfolds, and there on my left hand is a black glove made of synthetic weave, with a Velcro fastener. I hold up my gloved hand before my eyes. It is a miniature replica of the giant black glove that picked me up out of the ocean. There are several black wires that connect the glove to the arm of the dentist chair. I most certainly do not remember putting my hand in this glove.

Slightly disconcerted, but at the same time, growing used to unusual sights in this un-amusement park, I shed the black glove and head for the door. I step back into the hallway, closing the yellow door behind me. At the moment of re-entry, the hallway seems ordinary compared to my virtual reality experience. I feel a lump resting on my upper leg, in the right pocket. It must be my cell phone. I reach for it, with every intention of phoning anybody capable of getting me out of here. I pull it out of my pocket, discovering that it is not a cell phone at all. It is the little girl's glass marble. I'm tempted to roll the thing down the hallway. My second inclination is to keep hold of it. I conclude, for now, that my second instinct is the better one, and place it back in my pocket. It might come in handy, who knows?

SELF INFLICTED PLAGUE

I've grown accustomed to the hallway. There are fewer surprises here (unless, of course, I tamper with the mirror on the entry door). The hallway is quiet and dim and the doors stand at attention, like an endless row of soldiers, each of a different allegiance. I sit on the floor, midway between two doors, leaning back on the wall. Loneliness engulfs me like a self inflicted plague. I want to talk to a person I know, or reencounter a familiar face. I yearn to watch a movie with a friend. I miss the inane exchange of routine comments with a courtesy clerk at a supermarket. I feel so disengaged, detached, and unrelated to anything or anyone here. The little girl on the sailboat handed me a large white towel. It was, at least, a gesture of friendship, of humanity.

I pull the glass marble out of my pocket, and looking into it, hope to find the girl's face. The hallway is so dimly lit. There are muted lights on the wall, mounted at eye level. The lamps are frosted glass, shaped like seashells. They give off a soft amber glow. I hold up the glass marble to a hallway lamp, longing to see the girl's tiny features. I see only the pearly swirls of smoke. Perhaps the light is too low.

I contemplate the titles and nametags, the possessions and accomplishments that make me who I am. I have an address, I have a job. I have a small stash of money saved. I have a few hobbies, I like swimming and collecting old coins. I love museums and art exhibits. I have several friends. My roommate is a good friend. I telephone my mother, not often, but occasionally. Christmas presents and birthday presents always arrive early from my mother. I love coffee and watermelon and cashews. I love Chinese food and Mexican food. I love cats, but pets are not allowed where I currently live. I'm not merely a phantom stuck in a hallway. I am a real person with a real life. Or so I believe. The thought of my real life seems uneventful, even vacant, now seen from my current and removed perspective.   Perhaps, on second thought, I was somewhat of a phantom before I arrived here. "Nonsense," I say aloud. I am a rational, sensible, reasonable, and sane human being. You can't say that for every Tom, Dick, and Harry on the bus. Unfortunately, recollections of my life before I entered this hallway are not relieving my loneliness.

I scramble to my feet, prepared to select the next door. Truthfully, my heart is not in it. My spirit is sinking, and I sense a grudge, gaining momentum. I saunter down the hallway, noting the new door colors. Periwinkle, mango, emerald, vermillion, copper, charcoal (the interior decorator has gotten more sophisticated). I pause a moment, and consider sitting down again. I could take a nap, but I'm not sure where. Unexpectedly, the vermillion door opens, and a teenage boy steps out into the hall. He looks perhaps thirteen or fourteen. He's wearing square-rimmed glasses and a yellow and burgundy striped T-shirt. His baggy black jeans are rolled up to form cuffs over his white tennis shoes. In one hand he holds a battered skateboard, in the other is a silver chain that disappears into his pant's pocket. His white baseball cap has a yellow Z on it.

"New here, aren't ya?" He's chewing gum and his jawbone is etched with scruffy hair in the style of a leprechaun. His dishwater-blond hair bristles out from his ball cap, attempting to cover his ears.

"I guess you could say that."

"You wouldn't happen to be carrying a video camera would you?"

"No, I'm sorry, no camera of any sort on me."

"Bummer, dude. I was video-taping some skateboard stunts on the front-porch banister when the little guy opened the front door. He gave me the "come-here" finger. I was about to run off down the street, but something changed my mind. This house has always caught my eye, and I wanted to see the inside. I figured I could still run out the front door. The entry room was a trip, with the broken down Laughing Lady and the old mirrors. I must have set down the video camera before the goofy little dude opened the next door. After some of the weird stuff I've seen in here, I sure wish I had my video camera with me."

"I know what you mean. Have you been in here long?"

The kid rolls his eyes and scuffs the floor with his tennis-shoe toe. "It seems like days now. I've already fallen asleep about four or five times now. How about you?"

"I think I've been in here a few hours now. Have you gone for days without food?"

"Dude! Haven't you gone in the room with the gold door yet?"

"Not yet. Should I?"

"Are you kidding? There's enough food in there for a whole army, maybe for about a hundred armies."

"How do you get in? I have the whole ring of keys"

The boy pulls his silver chain and another ring of skeleton keys appears from his pants pocket.

"Whoa, I thought I had the only key ring for the whole place." Now I realize that the boy recognized me as an "outsider" by spotting the hoop of keys on my belt.

"We're not the only ones."

"You've encountered others?"

"Yeah. There's an old dude and a little girl. There's another kid about my age, but he's a freak."

"There's three other people in here with keys?"

"Hey, I met three of them, but it's hard to say. I know for a fact that you can get lost behind a door for an awful long time. Maybe some people are goners for good."

"That's a grim thought, but I don't doubt it."

"Are you hungry, dude?"

"Depends on what's on the menu."

"The chow is killer, man."

"That's what I'm afraid of."

"No, dude, not like that. I mean the food is stellar, like OUTSTANDING. Come on, check it out."

We walk back in the direction of the mirror. The kid slams his skateboard to the floor and jumps on. The rollers on the wood create a loud, cavernous, reverberated roar in the corridor. The sound stops abruptly and he flips the skateboard up with his toe, and catches it under his arm on his hip. It takes him no time to select the correct key, and with the gold door pushed slightly ajar, he waits for me to catch up. He bows deeply, and sways his hand in a low arch, like a doorman of a king's court. I enter regally upon a candlelit room. A long elegant table is laid out in a cornucopia feast, as if Louis XIV were about to arrive. The excessive abundance of cooked animals, fruit, and oven-hot breads, surrounded by arrays of thick sauces and vegetables, literally spill over the edges of the table. Trampled food litters the floor surrounding the entire length of the fare. Three grand arched windows loftily divide a cold stone wall. Gold embroidered curtains of silk and fine thread, descend from a height of perhaps thirty feet. The curtains are fringed and tasseled. Soft golden light feebly filters into the candlelit room. The candelabras on the table are grandiose. Thick white candles stand deformed, dribbling mounds of wax upon the central-most displays of edible delicacies.

At each end of the banquet, stretching the full length of a decent sized church, there stand two helmeted suits of armor. Each armored soldier stands unidentified, his right arm outstretched, grasping a long-handled halberd, with ax-like blade and a steel spike. The ax blade forms a half-circle. Surely, there are no men inside the suits of armor. I hope not.

The teenage skateboarder scarfs down a charred leg of duck, after tearing it from the bird's body with a sharp twist. I point, on the sly, to the suit of armor behind him and twist my lip to relay my unspoken concern. The teenager, still gobbling his drumstick, turns around and knocks on soldier's armored chest. There is a hollow banging sound. "Nobody home," declares the kid, reaching for a succulent peach. I would so much like to sit down and dine like a nobleman, but there's not a chair in sight. I take small samples of this and that. A grilled swordfish lies mortified upon an ornamental silver tray. Its scaly skin, dead eye, long sword, and shining fins, all remain intact. The eye seems to be observing me, so I opt for some warm bread and sharp white cheese. I slice an apple with what appears to be ruby-studded dagger. The mess on the floor is slimy, and I nearly slip and fall twice. If I were to gorge myself like the kid, I would surly have a stomach ache, so I limit myself to small tastes. I decide to hide an orange in my pocket. Skateboard Boy catches me in the act, and stuffs a hard roll into his pocket. His cheeks are packed like a chipmunk. He smiles at me, stretching his lips comically.

"Where do you sleep in this insane place?"
"Oh, you haven't tried the purple door, have you?"
"Not yet," I reply, still chewing on a piece of cheese.
He picks up his skateboard that he had leaned against the suit of armor. "Come on, you've got to see this one."

THE PURPLE DOOR

With both arms raised for support, the teenager balances his skateboard on his head. We mosey down the corridor. I'm feeling revived from the tidbits I've consumed. The boy has gained some distance ahead of me. When he steps on the Plexiglas aquarium in the floor, I can see that he is lit up from below. He stops to kneel down on the glass, "Hey, dude, check this out."

He's only a few doors ahead of me. I pick up my pace, but stop at the edge of the glass floor. I don't really trust the weight of the two of us on the aquarium glass. Normally, there are safety standards in public places, even private residences. I strongly doubt that this madhouse is government funded, or under the jurisdiction of a city zoning code. This location seems to be out of reach for the long hand of the law. (At this insight, I'm not sure whether to feel distressed or relieved.)

I kneel down on the floor to peer down into the aquarium. There is an iridescent green and purple fish swirling and darting about in the water amongst the seaweed. As it swoops nearer to the glass directly beneath us I see that it is not a fish, but a small bird, a swallow. Its shape is so aerodynamic, like an airplane from the era of art deco. Little bubbles leak from the bird's beak. How it can hold its breath for so long? The iridescent swallow darts in loop-to-loops as if performing for us. I wonder if there are tiny creatures in the water that the bird is feeding on by means of its rapid attack, or if the poor creature is seeking a way out of the tank.

"Come on," says the kid, in a tone that denotes his seniority and experience over me.

We head further down the hall toward the purple door.

"I want to show you something about the key for the purple door." The teenager sets down his skateboard, placing a foot on it to keep it from rolling away. Next, he pulls the chain on his belt. The key ring pops out of his pocket. He holds the ring up to a seashell light fixture on the wall, his finger feeling the tips of the keys.

"This one." He holds it up for me to inspect. "See how the teeth that interface with the lock are very thin on this key?" He grabs the key that he's referring to, gives himself a gentle push, and starts rolling down the hall on the skateboard. About three doors down, he stops with his flourished manner of flipping the skateboard up off the ground, catching it with his spare hand. He tucks the board under his arm, and with the other hand, turns the lock in the key. "Presto! Change-O! It's the only key that looks like that," he remarks with pride.

We step into a circular room. The room's floor gently rotates. With my first step onto the floor, I discover that the floor is circling to the left (clockwise). The walls create a dome, as if we were inside a small planetarium. The whole dome is lit up with a soft golden light, mixed with foggy swirls of orange and pink, creating a sky at sunset. The sunset is inaccurate. The sky is lacking east and west. The east would already have darkened while the west would be lit by a setting sun. Instead, the entire fishbowl above us is lit with the light of a setting sun.

In the center of the circular room, is a circular bed with a purple bedspread. The bed is gently circling to the right (counter-clockwise). "The bed is very comfortable, but I've had some intense dreams in here, and two horrifying nightmares," warns the boy.

"Everything about this whole place is like a weird dream, if you ask me," I note.

"No kidding."

"I think I'll lie down for a couple minutes."

"Suit yourself, I'll be seeing you around, dude." The teenager turns for the door.

"Wait, don't leave yet. Maybe we should stick together, it's better than going it alone.
Don't you think?"

"Sounds like a plan."

"You can lie down on the bed, too, if you want."

"Hey, dude, I'm not gay, O.K?"

"That's not what I'm saying, I'm not gay either. It's a big bed and there's plenty of room. We could talk some more."

"Thanks, but I don't get in bed with other dudes. I can stick around and talk though."

He sits down on his skateboard, cross-legged. The pose reminds me of Buddha, and I anticipate a philosophical discussion.

I lie back on the bed (there's a circular pillow in the middle). I can now see that the conversation might feel comical with me rotating in one direction, and the skateboarder circling around me in the other.

"So what should we talk about?" he asks me.

"That's a good question," I admit. I pause to think about the situation. "Have you ever seen the cooks who prepare the food for the banquet table behind the gold door?"

"That's a weird thing, dude. Every time I go in there to Mac out, I never see anyone else. There's always new food, but the room is always empty. I have a theory about that. I think that the room is *Food for the Dead.* I always heard that dead people are hungry. In some countries people believe that putting flowers on a grave is not enough. They actually leave food on the graves so the dead people won't get restless and come back to disturb the living. I was thinking this, because I thought, maybe I died and this is where I ended up. It's definitely not heaven, but it's not exactly hell. It's more like someplace in between. I was thinking - maybe when I was skateboarding in front of this house, doing stunts on the banister, maybe I fell and broke my neck. If that's what happened, then maybe the dorky little guy who signaled with his finger to "come here" was the Grim Reaper. He gave me these keys. They're not exactly the keys to the kingdom, but maybe they are the keys to my afterlife. Do you think something happened to you and now you are dead, too?"

"That thought hadn't occurred to me." (I diplomatically decided to withhold my theory about the dentist experimenting with virtual reality.) "But something has caught my attention when you were telling me about the front porch and the banister. I don't remember seeing the front of this house from the outside at all! What I do remember is being in a bookstore, looking through shelves of book. I had picked a book out that warned me that I shouldn't have come here. That was the very first sentence, I believe, "You shouldn't have come here." Well, it was just a book, telling me to not read further. The first page even advised that I put the book back and misplace it. I must have a rebellious tendency, or at least a curious nature. So, of course, I read on. I don't ever remember stepping from outside this house to the inside, but the "dorky little man" (as you so aptly put it) ushered me past the entry room with the laughing lady, then opened another door that opened onto the end of the hallway. I have not yet perceived that I am dead or that the little man was the Grim Reaper. Maybe he was the author of this book, and he has welcomed us into his imagination. These keys could be the keys to his imagination. The banquet room is *food for thought*. Just an idea, really, but if these rooms are his imagination, he has one warped imagination, if you ask me."

"Maybe you got mugged and murdered in the bookstore. Did you think of that one, dude?"

"I hadn't thought of that."

"Well, I hope you're right and the dorky guy is the author, because I don't really want to be dead and stuck in here, do you know what I mean?"

"Believe me, I don't want to be stuck in here either. I'm feeling sort of sleepy, but I still think it's a good idea for us to not separate. If I fall asleep, I'm afraid you'll wander off, and I'll be stuck here alone again."

"Don't worry, I'll stick around. Go ahead and take a nap, but don't blame me if you have a really sick nightmare." They teenager stretches out on the floor, using the skateboard as a pillow.

"Do you want to use the pillow," I offer.

"Nah, I'm fine."

I lie there like a clock's second hand circling the wrong way, and the teenager circles outside me like a logo on an automobile tire. Once again, I feel as though I'm being protected by a youngster. I nod off in no time.

MY FIRST PURPLE ROOM DREAM

A damp, threatening sky hangs like a charred weeping willow, casting a late afternoon gloom charged with presentiment. I am filled with a sense of marvel, as if entering Disneyland's Haunted House, an excitement mixed with apprehensive curiosity. A mosaic of dull colored millstones, cumbersome, and massive, forms two broad footpaths. Both paths lead to archaic semi-domes that house heavy splintering doors of the forbidding fortress. From a crowd of crawling children, I peer at the granite façade. Visible through the third-floor balustrade, animated youngsters, flock noisily from door to door. The children's voices are keyed up and enthusiastic. You would guess that they were at a carnival funhouse, but the fortress shelters the chambers of Japanese Wizards. Being wizards, their home appears quite medieval.

Those of us in queue for entrance already sense inklings of self-transformation. We are altered, perhaps bewitched. The suspense is horrifying, but surely we anticipate white magic, nothing morbid. With a clouded sense of trust, we proceed without inclination of turning back.

I am a teenager. Have I turned into the Skateboard Kid? All the other participants are younger, eight or nine years old. We crawl on the cold stones, although most of us have resorted to lying on our bellies, with our feet sticking up behind us. We wait our turns to enter. The first tactile evidence of the location's wizardry is felt on our arms and legs and bellies. The rows of grass blades, sprouting between the millstones of the footpaths, move as if on tiny rollers through narrow streets, tickling us with their feathery blade-tops.

Up ahead of our gathering of youngsters, we see children scramble to their feet as the heavy doors open upon glimpses of two of the wizards inside. The two wizards are dressed in the sheen and shine of white satin gowns. Their long, raven black hair is pulled back tight into a roll on top of each head. An X of two chopsticks holds the hair in place. With wry smiles, they stand in an elegant foyer of potted ferns surrounding a splendid trickling fountain of tiny tiles. In a soothing Zen simplicity on a checkered floor of huge tiles, stylized dwarf shrubs mark measured intervals throughout the room. A spiral staircase invites the children to ascend. The foyer is so dimly lit that the interior light resembles the exterior's sunless gray.

I wonder if I actually witness so much detail of the entry room, seeing that I remain in crab position on the bristling grass and damp millstones. I apparently have developed a visionary eye. Being so much larger than the rest of the children, I feel uninvited to this extravaganza. Maybe entry is exclusively for children under twelve. I feed overanxious, as though I missed out on the elated bustling for the third-floor doors. The little girl from the playground and sailboat is on the third floor now. Somehow I know, and I realize, too, that something sinister is going on up there. Since when have I become so extra-sensory perceptive?

There is a lapse in time combined with a lapse in memory. Did I fall asleep? I have, by some unknown means, been admitted to the Wizard's Fortress with the other children. As if waking from anesthesia, I don't recall actually passing through the enormous door. A phenomenal transformation has evolved. I am bobbing on gentle ocean-like waves with the other children. Each child, like a tree in an orchard, has plenty of water space. The waves swell and fall lugubriously, like the gentle water far from shore, before the surf curls under and breaks into waves. Each child clings to a carnivalesk, circus-like object. One pudgy boy holds onto the spiraled pole of a merry-go-round horse. A freckled girl in braids rides atop of a small dog house, and a sleepy looking boy with a shaved head is seated behind the small steering wheel of a bumper car. He looks car sick. A self-assured looking girl with long, blond hair rides a toppled-over rocking chair designed as a swan. She has her arms wrapped tightly around the swan's neck, and the swan's head ducks under water as if spying for a tasty fish. There is one overly stout girl wearing a chef's cap. The stout girl has draped her upper body over a gargantuan wooden spoon that floats as nicely as a log. Unfortunately for her, the spoon rolls in the water like a log would, and she's getting her exercise. I alternate between floating on my back and the dog paddle, without the assistance of any theatrical prop in the green water. That I lack a floating toy, only reminds me that I am older. Perhaps I was shooed into the fortress without a proper reservation.

Gently, the harmless waves begin to break on a sandy shore, where they fizzle and fade and dwindle to nothing. A vanishing ocean is one sure sign that the whole bobbing-in-water experience was entirely the manipulation of wizard's magic.

I find myself lying on the floor of a yellow room that is ill-formed, slanted, and askew. The wall to my left is taller than the wall on my right. The wall in front of me forms a trapezoid, and the floor is tilted like an inclined driveway. I'm lacking equilibrium from all the bobbing in the ocean. A tall door to the left opens. An oriental girl enters the slanted room, wearing a white chiffon party dress. Her tiny black shoes sparkle, and her straight black hair looks immaculately combed and shiny clean. As prim as a doll, she walks with her hands folded and resting on her flowering gown. A Japanese man's voice directs the small child in English. The accent is distinctly Japanese, "Go to the door across the room." The poor child sees me lying on the floor, and I surmise, by the look on her restrained face, that she has mistaken me for a dead body on the floor. I now perceive this room as terrifying. The voice is giving more directions, "Go forth and meet your death." Without hesitation, or altering her pace, the girl exits through the short door in the smaller wall. She leaves the door wide open.

I fear for the life of the doll-like girl. From the open door, an odd apparatus (perhaps an unfinished scarecrow) appears in the doorway. I see what looks like a mop with a small red rubber handball attached to the top of the handle. At the neck of the mop stick, just below the red ball is a fake black cape. The pitiful cape, made of plastic, perhaps a trash bag, fans out from the ball, lacking style or fashion altogether. The mop with the small red head, and its make-do, black cape crosses the room toward me. I am now standing up to defend myself. The mop tips its red head downward, as if bowing to me. I raise my hand to push it away, only to feel my hand turn wet and slimy, as if a dog had licked it. I jerk my arm back, and the mop in the garbage bag backs off.

It instantly occurs to me that it is I who has just met my death, and not the little girl who exited the room. I had shook hands with death, as simply as if I had met a new co-worker. It also occurs to me that this is one of the rooms on the third floor.   I had watched the children, bustling and anxious to enter this room. But I was not ushered through the third floor veranda, like the other children. The Wizards wanted to use me as a prop in the tilted yellow room. I was placed on the floor to frighten the youngster who entered.

Confusion overtakes reason.   The wizards have scrambling time. Something tells me that the children who enter this deformed yellow room will exit the door in the shorter wall and find themselves bobbing in the ocean with carnival toys.   I am experiencing everything out of sequence.

I begin to moan and groan in frustration. I feel a hand tugging my sleeve and wake up.   The teenage skateboarder has tugged on my shirt to wake me. "Hey dude, wake up. You started making weird sounds and I figured you were headed for a bad trip."

"I think I had already arrived at a 'bad trip'. Thanks for waking me."

"No sweat, dude. Get up. Let's get out of here."

Normally, I'm not big on someone less than half my age ordering me around. But so far, it seems to sit well with me. "OK," I reply, sitting up, feeling a little disoriented in the purple bed. The dome shaped sunset serves equally well as a sunrise. "How clever," I think to myself. However odd my dream was, I feel a sense of relief waking up in this revolving room.

GODDESS LADY AND THE SHOWERS

We exit the revolving room behind the purple door. The teenager places the skateboard on the hallway floor, prepared to push off, rolling elsewhere. I recount a condensed version of my dream for him. In response he empathizes, "Sounds pretty out there, dude." I explain that the part about having my hand slimed by the caped mop was unpleasant, but the thought that my hand had felt Death was not entirely alarming to me.

"You don't have to put on any brave act for me," the teenager adds. "My first dream in the purple room started out like a dream come true, but it got really gnarly, and ended up freaking me out totally."

"What was your dream about?"

"I didn't realize I had fallen asleep at first. I thought a spider had crawled across my pillow and into my hair, but when I opened my eyes, a gorgeous woman, really hot, was running her fingers through my hair. As she started taking off my clothes, more women started gathering around the purple bed. They were humming the letter M. At first it was a few women holding one note, but then new ones started in with another harmony note. By the time the hot lady in bed had me completely undressed, we were surrounded by naked women, all babes, who were holding hands and humming in twenty or thirty part harmony. The circle of women moved to the right on the rotating floor, while the bed circled to the left, with the incredible looking lady seducing me. I felt so excited to be having sex with this Goddess-like woman, and I figured that the other women were all waiting for their turns to be with me, which was all right by me, if you know what I mean.

Something started going wrong. The sex started getting too freaky. The Goddess lady tightened her thighs like scissors. She clamped down so tight on me, it felt like she would rip out my whole crotch. Her fingers sank into my back like giant pinchers and her kisses pierced my lips. She turned into a giant insect on top of me. Seriously, dude! I was surrounded by a circle of female insects all drooling to pull me apart. Now I know how a Thanksgiving turkey must feel. The monster insect lady ripped my sex organs right out of my crotch. I tried to scream bloody murder, but with my mouth in her grip, I could bare whimper. Up until then, I thought a toothache was the worst torture I had ever endured. I cannot begin to explain the pain, and there was so much blood oozing out of my pierced lips that all I could see was red. My eyes were full of blood, which was probably better than looking at the monster locked onto my face. I felt totally panicked, being pulled apart and unable to scream, while my whole mouth was clenched in the saw-toothed grip of the Goddess Insect's kiss."

"That's too scary for me," I had to admit.

"Yeah. That's what I say, and thanks for not saying what the old dude told me, 'You shouldn't have been messin' around with under-aged sex,' like I could control what I dreamed!"

"I thought you said that she was a woman."

"He was talking about me. I'm not even sixteen yet."

We are both standing out in the hallway, discussing our purple room dreams. I notice, as we talk, a putrid smell like a dead animal, something rotten mixed with the smell of urine. I discover that the smell diminishes whenever the kid rolls away a few feet on his skateboard. I can't really blame a young kid for forgetting personal hygiene in a place like this. He's been here a lot longer than me. I'm getting a headache myself, and could really use a cup of coffee, not to mention the relief of a bathroom. The kid is down the hall trying out stunts on his skateboard.

"I have three questions," I call out to the kid.

"Fire away," he yells back without looking back.

"One, is there a restroom in this place? Two, have you run across a pot of coffee anywhere? And three, what if I want to take a shower?"

The teenager makes a U-turn and heads back toward me. "There's a fancy urn of hot coffee on the banquet table behind the gold door. Here, let me show you something the old dude taught me." He reaches up for the seashell shaped light fixture on the wall, pulls it down like a lever, and a hidden doorway within the wall swivels open. We step through the hidden door, into large room that looks like an old fashioned restroom at a train station. The tiles on the floor create a chicken-wire pattern and there are rows of urinals and toilet stalls. The slide latches on the doors of the stalls are broken. There's another row of sinks, shaped like birdbaths, in the middle of the room.

"No showers anywhere?" I enquire.

The teenager leads me to the end of a tile wall, and around the corner points to a row of shower heads and drains. There are so many showers that it reminds me of the hallway of doors, and I wonder if there isn't an army of soldiers somewhere that uses these showers. Despite the eerie sight of shower heads and shower drains lined up endlessly to a focal point horizon, I sense a bright cheerfulness about the shower room. Along the opposite tiled wall, above an endless row of towel hooks, there are ventilation windows. The narrow panes, hinged along the bottom, are braced with folding metal slats. These windows have been left open, leaving a space between the ceiling and the top of the window, wide enough for an arm to reach through. The glass is nearly opaque, and embedded with chicken wire. In the small triangular opening above the metal support arm, I glimpse lilac blossoms swaying in a light breeze. Beams of sunlight twirl between the crisscross of lilac branches and enter the tiny openings into the shower room. I hear a birdcall that repeats itself once. A second birdcall, a slight alteration of the first, is once again repeated, creating an ongoing sampling of different birdsongs.

I ask the kid to wait a couple minutes while I shower. I feel inclined to suggest that he takes a shower too, but I don't want him to think that I'm trying to get naked with him. I don't even want to offend him by letting him know that he smells, because he's been watching out for me and knows where things are. For now, I'll have to hope that if I set a good example, he will follow suit.

The teenager says he'll wait for me in the toilet room. I hear his skateboard on the tile floor as he circles the birdbath sinks. The bird continues to imitate the birdcalls of a series of birds. As I am undressing, it occurs to me that a mockingbird may have been named for this very reason, stealing the songs of every bird that he hears. I have stripped to my underwear, using the towel hooks to hang my clothes. The bird is now imitating car alarms, perhaps even a computer game. There seems to be a birdcall that sounds like a Nazi air-raid siren. Another birdcall reminds me of a mechanical frog.

I turn on the shower and adjust the temperature. The bar of soap on the ledge is used, but it looks clean. What a relief to rinse off the stickiness that clings to my skin like a mummy wrap. The warm water relaxes my tense shoulders. The fizzle of water spray splashing the floor tiles muffles the sound of the skateboard in the other room and the mockingbird out the window. By the time I've rinsed and turned off the water the mockingbird is silent and so is the teenager. I call out to him, and I realize that I don't even know his name. "Are you still over there?" My voice creates a slight echo.

"Yeah, I'm just zoning out. Hurry up, will ya?"

"Hold on to your horses. You've got an important date or something?"

"Nah, I just want to get out of here."

"O.K."

As I'm dressing I hear far off metallic tones out the window. There is a muffled rhythm to the intonations. They resemble female voices reverberated through a sewer pipe. There is a lighthearted singsong to the inflections. The voices sound almost wet, like water drops. I cannot make out a single word, but I make a guess that two teenage girls are calling out to each other in a parking complex.

"Can you hear those voices?" I call out to the teenager.

"No. What voices?"

I peek around the edge of the divider between the showers and the restroom. He's sitting on his skateboard with his head leaning up against the wall. "Come over here by the window and listen."

"Are you dressed yet?"

"Everything but my shoes." This kid seems really intimidated by me, or by men, I'm thinking.

The kid picks up his skateboard and walks into the shower room. We both look up at the windows and wait for any reoccurring noise. Faintly, I hear a squealing sound, followed by what must be a sassy comeback, but still there are no distinguishable words.

"Maybe it's the Laughing Lady," he suggests.

"Maybe this is our way out of here," I point out.

"That's what I used to think." The kid smirks at me. "I think you need to see this for yourself."

The kid makes a foot lock with his hands and offers to boost me up so I can see out the edge of the window. "Grab hold of the ledge, you're too heavy for me." I pull myself up with my arms as he holds me up by the foot. Just a foot away, on the other side of the lilac blooms there is an impressive coil of barbed wire. The spikes on the wire are like sharpened razors, like the wire you see on prison walls.

"Those wires can be cut with wire cutters." I inform him.

"Been there, done that," the kid tells me in a deadpan tone of voice. "I'll tell you what happened to me when I tried to get out through these windows, but first things first. I'm getting really hungry. Let's go back to the banquet room, and I'll tell you the whole story after we eat something."

"Sounds like a plan." This kid sure knows how to take control.

ATTEMPTED ESCAPE

The coffee in the banquet room is fresh and strong. Who made it? Maybe the story is the reverse of my theory about *Food for the Dead.* Maybe this food is prepared by the dead for the living souls trapped in this asylum. Not far off from *Food for Thought,* but more precisely, *Food for the Brain,* or *Food for the Warped Mind.* There is no artificial sweetener for my coffee, only sugar cubes and honey. I drink out of a goblet, and the last few sips of coffee taste metallic. This time I sample the smoked ham and deep purple globe grapes. A light bulb flashes above my head in a cartoon balloon, "Maybe I'm not really here. This is only my imagination or a long, drawn out dream. Maybe I've been drugged with sleeping pills and I'm sleeping for a whole week. If this is not real, I can eat anything I want." I help myself to two desserts, bread pudding and chocolate éclairs.

The teenager is wolfing down a large drumstick again. I play the part of concerned parent and suggest that he try some vegetables with that. "Practice what you preach, buddy. The green stuff is decoration if you ask me," he barks back.

"Point well taken." I select some green beans and asparagus, and they taste sumptuous after the overload of sweets. "Mmmm," I purr with relish. The teenager looks at me out of the sides of his eyes, as if to convey, "Don't try coercing me."

He tells me his escape attempt story, being captured by agents who threatened to enlist him in the army to join the war effort. *"I carry a hunting knife inside my pant leg. The knife worked as a screwdriver for unfastening the window braces, but I was unable to cut the wire. The sharp thorns of the barb wire were too long. I did discover that if I stabbed the knife into the flower branch, I could suspend the coil of wire on the end of the knife handle. This widened a space between the wall outside the window and the thorny coiled wire. I managed to lower myself from the window with only a few rips on the backside of my jeans* and a couple scrapes on my back shoulder. The drop to the ground was about fifteen feet. After most of the freaky stuff I'd been through in here, I didn't have as much fear of heights as I usually do. As soon as I hit the ground I fell backward. An alarm went off that reminded me of the bell at school. Three guards stepped away from the sidewalk (you can't really see the sidewalk below the windows because there's not enough space to stick your head out the shower room windows). The guards were dressed in white and silver. They looked all perfect and handsome, like the kind of guys that girls go nuts over. They had silver colored baseball bats in their hands. Aluminum bats are bad news to get clobbered with. I saw some punk break my big brother's arm once with an aluminum baseball bat. The only difference with the guards, here, the metal bats are small, like billy clubs carried by the Keystone Cops. I thought size was the only difference 'til one guard pointed his club at a geranium plant at the edge of the sidewalk. A red laser beam, emanating from his aluminum club, fried the geranium to a black stick. Getting fried looked like worse pain than having my private parts ripped out by the Insect Goddess. I decided not to run for it, the guard might turn me to toast. I did precisely what the three dudes told me to do.

They formed a triangle of bodyguards around me and escorted me back into the building through a side entrance. There are lots of side entrances here. The side of the building looks like the Wall of China from the outside. As you can imagine, there are lots of guards. I figured out that's why there are so many showers. Anyway, the guards walked me into a room with a lightbulb hanging from a cord over a card table with two folding chairs. Two new guys in white dress suits entered the room. One was chubby with black rimmed rectangular glasses hanging on the end of his nose. The chubby guy had a clipboard in his hand against his hip. The other guy was slender, with a severe haircut. He had a long face and pitted skin from bad acne. His straight brown hair was slicked down with a part on the side, and a swoop of his plastered hair covered one eyebrow. It wasn't plastered good enough, 'cause it kept falling over one eye. His greasy black hair was cut in a shape like a bowl had been placed on his head. One penetrating eyeball peered out at me with a mean look, like he was daring me to tell just one, itsy bitsy lie. They say a master looks like his pet dog. I would put this guy with a Doberman pinscher. He warned me that I must cooperate fully if I didn't want to be sent overseas to join the war effort. Mr. One-Eyed Doberman would ask questions while the chubby guy made check marks on his clipboard. An extra guard had joined the three that ushered me in, making a guard for each corner of the small room. "What's your name?" Mr. Doberman would fire at me. "Where do you live? Why are you here? Did anybody tell you about this compound? Have you contacted any outsiders? What rooms have you entered? Who have you talked to here? What did they tell you? What did you tell them?" I would answer the questions quickly, so as to not arouse suspicion. I looked directly at Mr. Doberman, because I wanted him to believe my answers. I was scared out of my wits, but I did my best to not let it show. I had to pee like crazy, but I didn't dare mention it. He definitely did not look like the type of guy who allowed restroom passes.

I need to let you know some extra information that really had me sweating big time. My older brother has served in the military and was sent overseas for active duty. Since his return home, he has told me stories about how bad things got over there. Most of it was gory tales about being shot at, about car bombs, or about raiding buildings and finding innocent civilians injured or dead, or babies with their heads blown off. That stuff was disturbing enough, but he also knew a couple prisoners of war. One was released and the other must have escaped. The prisoners were submitted to daily interrogations. If the answers were insufficient, or unsatisfactory, a finger was chopped off the guy's hand, one finger per day. One of his buddies returned home with two stubs for hands. The poor guy knew of another guy who lost all his toes in addition to the severed fingers.

Needless to say, I took the interrogation process very seriously. As you know, this place is whacky enough, and now I figured that a consensus, concerning my proper punishment, would have to be decided. After what seemed like a half an hour of intensive questioning, I was lead out of the room. The dudes in the white dress suits did not leave the room. The four guards stood at attention facing me in the hallway. Not only did I expect to pee my pants, I began to suspect that I had diarrhea. Simultaneously, the four guards saluted me. They turned and entered the room, leaving me standing alone in the hall. I wanted to reach for the seashell lamp and open the restroom door, but it was too late. I wet my pants.

A short moment passed. Nobody came out of the room, so I reached for the seashell hallway light. The restroom door opened and I ran into a stall to relieve myself. My pants were soaked, and I needed to take a shower. One thing I don't like is the idea of getting caught naked in here by whomever or whatever might just drop in, so I took a shower with my clothes on. I didn't dare close my eyes or wash my hair, because I expected the guards to come storming into the shower room and drag me out. I dried off as quickly as I could, but I dripped water everywhere I walked and my tennis shoes sounded like suction cups on squeaky glass. I was concerned that my hunting knife would rust, so I wrapped it up in a dry towel. I carried it in one hand and the skateboard in the other. I found my skateboard in the shower room, right where I had left it, directly under the window I had climbed out earlier.

I poked my head out into the hallway and the coast was clear, so I headed straight for the silver door. If the guards wanted to track me down, all they had to do was follow the trail of water I left on the floor. Have you opened the silver door yet?"

"No, not yet."

"Dude! You have some real catching up to do. The silver door is your passport to a tropical vacation. I went straight to the silver door, and stretched out on the sand in the sun. I unfolded the towel around my hunting knife, and spread it out on the sand like a beach towel. I looked up at the tallest palm trees I've ever seen in my life. I shielded my eyes from the bright sun, and gazed out at sparkling *turquoise water that rolled onto the white sand. It was paradise, dude, real paradise!"*

"Take me to paradise, then."

"Right on."

PARADISE

I've seen this exact palm lined beach on the cover of a travel brochure. I think the advertisement was for a vacation getaway to Barbados, an island country of the E. West Indies. Why hasn't the entire affluent population of the world flocked here? I'm lying here in the mid-afternoon glow, listening to the gentle surf and the spray of breakers. Down by the water, a smelly teenage boy is poking a long branch into the sand, in search of conch shells and sand dollars. He's left his skateboard beside me in the white sand, with the instructions, "Guard it with your life."

"I would take a bullet for your skateboard," I quipped.

The kid smiled, and I felt the first inklings of a sense of trust given me.

"Hey dude, wildlife sighting out at sea!" and he points his long stick off to the right. I sit up in time to witness four dolphins jumping effortlessly in arches as if there were hoops to jump through. I lean back on my elbows and within minutes a flock of pelicans fly low to the water, their wings beating in slow motion like pterodactyls. The kid lumbers up the slope of sand to where I sit. He's carrying his baseball cap. He plops down cross-legged, and empties out the little shells and sand dollars on his skateboard for display.

"Your skateboard tried to sneak away, but I warned it that I was keeping a hawk's eye on it."

"Thanks," the boy responds without looking up, without acknowledging any playfulness. In the last handful of shells pulled from his cap, there is a large glassy marble. I instantly suspect that the kid has picked my pocket. "Hey, let me see that marble you found." He tosses it to me without hesitation, and I'm guessing that he's developed a deft sensitivity for utilizing a poker face to cover his tracks.

I hold the marble up to the sunlight, and sure enough there are swirls of pearlescent smoke inside.

"How'd you get hold of my marble?" I ask with a suspicious tone.

"I've had that marble before I ever met you," the kid raises his voice defensively.

I prop myself up on my knees so as to reach into the right pocket of my pants. With dismay, I pull out my own glass marble. "Hey, I'm sorry. My mistake."

The kid looks at me with a disappointed smirk on his face. I feel that I've lost the little bit of trust that was developing. I hold both of the marbles up to the sun. The marble in my right hand looks nearly identical to the kid's marble. Within a half-second, the little girl's face appears in the swirl of smoke within the marble in my right hand. The little girl says, "Be careful." Her face looks concerned and she sounds as if she's scolding somebody.

"Did you hear that voice?" I ask the teenager.

"No, is my marble talking to you, too?"

"Actually, it was my marble."

"I didn't hear anything. Hand over your marble and I'll take a look."

I feel as though I'm handing over a precious treasure, a crystal ball, or a dream world computer. A strong instinct is grasping my gut. I don't really want to hand the boy this gift from the little girl, but I do. He holds my marble up to the sunlight. "I don't hear anything or see anything," he reports. He extends his hand to return my marble to me. I reach out my hand, and I freeze when I see the mirror image of myself standing before me, instead of the teenager. In an automatic reflex, I look down at my shoes. I'm not wearing my dress shoes. I'm wearing the kid's tennis shoes, which makes no sense, because my feet would not fit into his shoes. I look at my arms and realize that I have the arms of the teenage boy. "No way!" we both yell simultaneously.

I hear my own voice say something, but I have not voiced a single word, "We better trade marbles." There I am gesturing with my free hand, signaling to hand it over. "Trade marbles," my voice is saying again, without passing from my own lips. Of course the words are not passing from my lips. I am now the teenager. I take a deep breath, "O.K," and the kid's voice rises up from my lungs. I feel like screaming, but that would look ridiculous, so I hand over the marble to myself. This mirror of myself hands his marble to me, and we exchange marbles in one precise moment. I look down at my feet and I still see tennis shoes. I hold the marble up to the sunlight again, and I see my twin self doing the same. The little girl in the marble is yelling, "Be careful!" My arms now look like my own arms. I look down at my feet, and there are my dress shoes again. I touch my ears and my chest, and sure enough I am restored to myself again. Facing me now is the teenage kid. "Thank God," we now exclaim simultaneously. We both laugh.

"Well that added a strange twist to paradise!" I postulate.

"Tell me about it!" says the kid with a look of relief.

"Have you had enough of paradise?" the young lad jests.

"I almost hate to admit it," I reply. "Let's get out of here." I turn around. I can no longer see the doorway that we entered to step out onto this beach. "How do you get out of here?"

"I bet some of the goody-two-shoes that ended up in heaven are asking God the same question," the little guy interjects. "Don't worry, dude, we just trace our footsteps back through the sand."

We walk up the incline of beach, following our own footprints toward patches of whisper weed, where the white sand thins out. Abruptly, before we arrive at the weed patch, the footprints vanish. "Now what?" I wonder.

The brainchild lifts an index finger, makes a low bow, and waves me past him. However satirical, I enjoy his treating me like royalty, so I walk onto the untouched sand. My hard-soled shoes clomp down on a hardwood floor, jarring my brain as I absorb a familiar sight, the endless hallway. I feel as if I'm wearing wooden clogs from the Netherlands. The sound of my shoe echoes down the hallway, followed by the muted squeak of the teenager's rubber sole scuffing the varnished floor behind me.

"Where's your skateboard?" I ask with feigned alarm.

The kid opens his eyes wide, "Back to paradise we go." He does an about-face, and I now see his skateboard held behind him.

"Wise guy," I squint my eyes in adlibbed anger. He turns to face me, pretending to prepare for my wrath, raising his shoulders and pulling back his face with gritted teeth to avoid my explosion of irritation.

There is no explosion of anger. I merely raise a hand in surrender and ask him about his glass marble. "So you have a little girl in your marble who talks to you, too?"

He looks puzzled. "Who said it was a little girl? It's the old dude's face in my marble. He has a long gray beard and a bald head. He wears little round reading glasses."

"What does he tell you?"

"Stupid stuff, like he thinks he's my grandfather or something."

"Stupid stuff like what, for example?" I probe.

"Instead of yelling at me like my dad always does, he gives me these dumb little tidbits of thought-provoking advice. The trouble is, I know all his advice already."

"That still doesn't tell me what he says," I point out.

"O.K, O.K, he keeps repeating the same thing over and over, like a skipped C.D. He says, 'Don't react, stop and think. Before you act, think, think, and then think some more.' He must be talking to somebody else, because I already do this."

I had the same feeling when the little girl in my marble warned, "Be careful." I thought she was yelling at her younger brother or somebody else. Come to think of it, though, I was in the midst of exchanging marbles with the wiz kid, and I had no idea we would end up exchanging identities (not to mention bodies, minds, and souls). Did we actually exchange minds and souls? That might have been interesting.

"My marble was saying *be careful,* but it wasn't an old guy with a beard. It was a little girl that gave it to me on a sailboat. Did somebody give you your marble?"

The teenager puckers his lips like a fish. "The old dude gave me the marble after I fell into a trap door in the pink room."

"What's up with these talking marbles that people give us with their faces inside them? Are we being initiated into some secret society? Next thing you know, we'll start passing out glass marbles to newcomers here."

"That's deep, dude!"

I laugh at the kid's choice of words and he starts laughing, too.

"I think it's about time for a snack-a-roo in the banquet room. Care to join me for some pheasant under glass?" suggests the little wise guy.

"That's what I like, a man with a plan."

It has been advised to troubled souls that a family member (or close friend) can serve as a sounding board. If a person has a trusting relationship with any co-worker, schoolmate, or neighbor, the act of confiding in someone can serve as a highly economical alternative to visiting a therapist or psycho-analyst.

Apparently, our appetites had built to robust proportions. The brain child and I circle the table over and over, sampling meats and breads, cheeses and verdure, nuts, seeds, melons and berries. Food stains our fingers and chins with the hues of varied delicacies. We compare each others' histories. Who did we live with on the outside? Who did we love and who did we despise? What were our passions and pet-peeves?

My train of thought is locked into the conversation. Without conscious awareness of my behavior, I sample an array of desserts, leaving behind the tattered remains of at least ten descent servings. Among the damaged ruins are a parfait, a tart, a flambe, an eclair, and a sorbet enhanced zabaglione. Unknowingly, I have psychologically arrived at my very first *free meal* mode of dining. The teenager has long since thrown out such irrelevant etiquette as *finishing one's serving,* and, no doubt, the boy has not yet acquired any work-ethic guilt attached to the wasting of food. As we reveal our backgrounds to each other, we devour to our hearts content, feeling confident that the food, the experience, and the lavish presentation of the feast are all imagined. We are not in a waking reality of eating. We are, rather, trapped in a dream full of food.

"My dad is a certified jerk, and that's putting it mildly, compared to names my friends and my older sister come up with. I have some pretty déclassé names for him myself, but I have to admit that you seem like the mature, genteel type, who shies away from trashy name-calling. My dad deserves every single name we give him. He gets mad at everything, and if you do something right, or if you make a special achievement, he'll find some way to tear it down. He's done some really sick stuff to me, and I'm pretty sure that my older sister has gone through worse hell than me."

"What does he do to you?"

"I really don't want to talk about it. It's just depressing, and I don't even blink an eye or let-on about anything to anybody out there in the real world. If my dad ever found out that I squealed on him, he'd be on me like a hungry grizzly bear on a picnic basket. And who's going to believe me anyway? I have battle scars I could show you, but any kid can fall off his bike or his board and get banged up, you know what I mean?"

"He beats you?"

The boy stares a hole in the floor and then he finally says, "No comment. I already told you more than I ever told anybody, and that's because I don't even think you're real. You're probably just a part of my imagination like everything else in here."

"I know what you mean. I've thought the same thing about you, but not after your description of you dad. You seem like a real enough person to me, at least, at the moment. I have a life of my own outside of here. My life may be a little boring for some people, but I don't have my parents on my case, or any other serious trouble. I may have some serious problems now that I stepped into this madhouse, but my life before was fairly simple and easy going. I love fluffy cats and don't care much for large dogs."

"You can have your fluffy cats, dude. I like dogs, the bigger the better. Little yappy dogs get on my nerves, though. They're only good for old ladies. One thing I like about a dog is that he will watch out for you, and another thing is when you come home he'll come running up all happy to see you. Cats are creepy. They have those big reptile eyes that just stare straight at you with that annoying blank expression, like they are thinking, 'Who the heck are you, and who even cares?' They keep their distance, all selfish and uncaring. They're demonic if you ask me."

"O.K., Mr. Dog's Best Friend, you get all the big dogs we come across, and I'll keep all the fluffy cats."

"Deal," and he shakes my hand. "I sure wish we could just go to a movie theater with cokes and popcorn and watch a good flick. Instead, I feel like I'm stuck in some marathon movie. What kinds of movies do you like?"

"My usual idea of entertainment is a trip to a museum or an art exhibit, or maybe a movie with some social or psychological content to it. I could go for some swashbuckling adventure film if it's done creatively, or with a decent sense of humor. I'm not really big on slapstick, or cops and robbers, or the endless amount of *Let's-get-the-drug-dealer* movies. We've had a zillion of those on T.V. and the subject has been beaten to a dead horse by now."

"Sounds like you're the more refined, humanist type. When I go see a flick I want to see buildings exploding and cars crashing and people getting mutilated or brutally killed. What the world could use about now is a massive plague or a world war, anything to wipe out at least three fourths of the population. If you ask me there are too many greedy people already. They might put on an act like they're all concerned about the welfare of others, but if you watch them you can tell what the truth is. Most of them are heartless and they just want more stuff for themselves and for their own kids. Most people think like cavemen, except now they have better toys."

I smirk at his scathing commentary. "I had a pretty harsh opinion of the human race when I was a teenager. I've lightened up a lot over the years, though, and I discovered that a lot of people are capable of being generous and compassionate. You know what? I'm stuffing myself to the gills here, but to tell the truth, I'm starting to miss some good Chinese food or Mexican cooking. Don't even get me started about Thai food. I love Thai food."

"I could go for a big fat burrito - any day, anytime."

"Tell me about it."

"Dude, where do you live, on the outside, I mean?"

"I live in an apartment. I have one roommate. His name is Joseph. He's a little odd, but we get along. He loves to watch television and munch on potato chips or Cheetos, or onion flavored crackers, anything that makes a lot of noise. I pass through the living room as quick as possible, because he's usually stretched out on the couch, watching sitcoms or cartoons. I go shut myself in my own room and read, or else I go to a coffee house and read, or write out my bills, or just stare off into space and watch the human race; all the conglomeration of styles and mannerisms and varieties of speech "

"What kind of books do you read?"

"Contemporary fiction's my favorite, T. Coraghessan Boyle, or Margaret Atwood, or Barbara Kingsolver. I read authors from India or China, or someone like Naguib Mahfouz from Cairo, who gives me a glimpse of daily life in other countries. What about you?"

"Science fiction, pure science fiction is all you find in my room. I like the ones about evil children, or alternative universes, or stuff like medical advances that backfire and start making everyone cough up blood and hallucinate horrifying visions. Voodoo can be fun to read about, you know, putting an ugly curse on somebody?"

"Sounds like we have different tastes."

"Everyone does. Speaking of tastes, I love Mexican food, too. That's one thing we have in common. And being stuck in here, that makes two. If you ask me, Chinese food is kind of boring. You know what would be awesome? A big fat juicy hamburger cooked on a charcoal grill. I could eat about two truckloads of chips and salsa, and about five cheeseburgers with extra mustard, no sweat, dude. And pepperoni pizza! Are you kidding? I can just taste a blue Gatorade just about now. I mean, the food in here is really excellent gourmet cuisine and all that malarkey, but I miss some real food, you know? Hot dogs and greasy tacos and macaroni and cheese and some salty fries! There's no ketchup here, did you notice that?"

"I hadn't thought about it 'til you just now mentioned it."

"As far as where I live and who I live with – my house is a place where you don't want to go, trust me. I would go so far as to say that this place is better. It's kind of science fiction here if you think about it. The only problem is, it's a lot safer to read a book than live here. In a book, if the alien pulls off a part of your body, it sounds all cool and gory. But in here you have to feel everything that happens. That part about being here reminds me of being at home, which really sucks big time. One good thing at home is my CD collection. It was just starting to get really good and now I can't listen to any of 'em."

"What do you listen to?"

"The usual stuff, *Buckethead, SonicYouth, the Subdudes,* stuff like that. *The Pixies* have a great CD called *Wave of Mutilation,* and *Skinlab* has an awesome disc called *Skid Row."*

"Sounds inspiring."

"You can't beat old school *Metallica* for surfin' the cement."

"Makes me feel like a real old-timer."

"Hey, like Popeye says, 'I ams what I ams.' We all have our own drum to beat."

"Good point, Mr. Philosophy."

"You've got a whole bag full of names for me, don't you? You know, I have to agree with you about another thing. When it comes to the boob tube, I hate sitcoms and cartoons, too. Well, *The Simpsons* are O.K. I'd rather be checkin' out MTV, or if I have the *dinero,* I just go out and buy the CD and listen to it while I'm boarding around town. I don't even look forward to owning a car. There are too many automobiles already, if you ask me. I'd rather be riding my board."

"Hey, you're doing the environment a favor."

The teenager gives one thumb up in approval.

"I wish there was an espresso café in here somewhere," I comment, hoping my inflexion and tone sound offhanded. I don't want to sound like I'm complaining.

"You miss Starbucks. <u>Dude</u>, they've got you addicted!"

"Hey, I was addicted to coffee before I ever set foot into a Starbucks."

"I forgot how old you really are."

"Better old than dead, which is what you're going to be if you say that again."

The brainchild beams a delightful smile, his sign of approval at my dark humor. "Hey, dude, I've got an idea. Behind the orange door there is a reception room. I think it's a dentist, or a doctor, or a plastic surgeon, or something like that. Anyway, there are couches and magazines and there's a little table with a coffee pot and Styrofoam cups. I think they have those packages of cappuccino powder that you can mix with hot water."

"Let's take a look." It sounds a little dreary compared to what I had in mind, but we are stuck here in reduced circumstances, or should I say *induced circumstances*, or for all I know *expanded circumstances*. We exit the ravaged banquet-table room, and once again traverse the hallway, the skateboard growling on the floor planks and my dress shoes clicking quickly behind. Wafts of body odor trail behind the wiz kid. I'm beginning to wonder if my eyes will start watering, or if the stench will materialize visually as brownish-gray smoke clouds. "Hey Mr. Science, you might consider bathing any day now. The smell is getting a little too unbearable for me to endure."

The kid whirls around and around in a continuous pirouette on the back wheels of his skateboard. I begin to wonder if he is not a champion ice skater. He stops abruptly and theatrically, facing me, with his arm held high and his nose whiffing his armpit. "It is getting a little ripe, isn't it?"

"There is no shortage of showers, you know."

"I took a couple of showers in there, but that was before my little escape attempt out the bathroom window. Every since I met those laser-armed guards, I've had no desire to take off my clothes. Can you imagine being hauled into an interrogation room in your birthday suit?"

"I can imagine, and I sympathize with your precautionary stance, but believe me – I can also imagine giving my poor nose a break from your B.O."

"I could wash the armpits in the sink without removing my pants."

"You could go for a swim again in paradise, and dry out on the sand."

"That sounds kosher."

"Maybe you'd consider doing both," I say with raised eyebrows.

"It's that bad, huh?"

I nod my head and he smirks. "O.K., let's make a quick pit stop before we go to the doctor's office." He reaches for the frosted seashell lamp, and disappears through the swivel door. He reappears, at least halfway cleaned up, and we head for the orange door on a mission for powdered cappuccino. Once again we reach the aquarium glass in the floor. A white owl floats slowly across the dancing seaweed. The owl looks entirely at home in the water. I wonder at the sight of it how similar the two elements, air and water, really are. We stop, momentarily, to admire the hypnotic swaying of the seaweed. The white owl vanishes from our rectangular frame. Within seconds, three large ravens come spiraling across the water, like Blue Angels putting on an air show. The immense blackbirds are at once ominous and yet mesmerizing, and I can imagine a sinister waltz, like the music of a shamanistic circus, accompaniment to the spectacle.

We continue noisily down the corridor. At a door that I would either call faded salmon or cantaloupe, the kid starts sorting through his key ring. He selects the correct key, first try. What a showoff! Sure enough, the room looks exactly as he described – a generic waiting room with a receptionist's desk.

"Good afternoon, gentlemen," the receptionist greets us. "The Practitioner has two clients ahead of you. Please help yourself to the refreshments." She points to an end table beside a salmon colored couch. The receptionist's blouse matches the couch, except that her blouse has a silvery sheen to it. She wears rectangular black-framed reading glasses that rest on the rounded tip of her otherwise straight nose. Her face is round and puffy and somewhat pink. Her hair is almost comical, a helmet of thickly hair-sprayed jet-black bristles teased up from her left ear, swooping over her head like a cartoon ocean wave, and then curling up in a flip above her right ear. Her hairstyle is either retroactive or a wig borrowed from a drag queen. The word *practitioner* leaves me clueless as to service about to be rendered, and the word *client* brings to mind a question of payment. Up until now I had not considered whether or not I was carrying money in my pocket. I have gone without a single expense here at this Unamusement Park. I reach for my back pocket, and there is my wallet, as usual. Inside I discover seven dollars, a bank card, and a Discover card. I hold my breath until I locate my ID. Same old ID, same old address, 1440 Orange Grove Ave., Apt. #33. My photograph seems to have faded slightly, and it may be my imagination, but my face looks slightly as if it has begun to melt. Maybe the ID card got overheated somehow. The teenager continues looking at paintings on the wall, failing to check my ID to learn my name. I have to admit, I almost prefer not knowing his name. His name will give him a reality status, unlike anything else I've encountered here. I tuck my cards back into my wallet and stuff the wallet back into my back pocket.

The kid plops down on the salmon couch and I prepare a phony instant cappuccino. I sit beside the teenager. He has discovered a science fiction magazine called *Science Psyche*. At the first taste of frothy cappuccino, the kid remarks, "Dude, I just had a weird thought. What if this is a dream world uninterrupted. You know, like you and I don't have to bother going to sleep or waking up to get here. But that's not the weird part. What if this is reality and the true dream is what's going on outside. I mean, what makes the life that we knew before so real anyway? Can you honestly say that it all made sense, that we were actually achieving anything out there? What makes that world any more real than this world?"

"Actually I read about that idea once. It was pointed out to Carlos Castaneda by a Yaqui Indian in Mexico. For some reason I don't think the Yaqui Indians ever visited a place like this one, but who knows?"

"Dang it all to blankity-blank-blank. And I thought I was going to go down in history as some philosophical innovator. I hate it when I think up something new and then I find out somebody else already discovered it."

"Hey, don't be so quick to put yourself down. Who knows, you might be onto something really big. One thought leads to another and you could end up discovering the meaning of dreams or the meaning of life or any number of things."

"Maybe, like I'm discovering the meaninglessness of it all."

"Maybe you can get a Ph.D. in that."

"Very funny, Dr. Frankenstein."

I take another sip of my cappuccino and look at the wall hangings. There is a large outline of an eye, not unlike the Egyptian symbol. Perhaps the practitioner is an optometrist. There is an embroidered saying hanging next to the wall. The saying reads: WAR IS PEACE, FREEDOM IS SLAVERY, IGNORANCE IS STRENGTH. I nudged the wiz kid, absorbed in his *Science Psyche* magazine.

"That slogan reminds me of a book I read once."

"I think it was George Orwell, 1984. I had to read that it last year for a class. It's kind of creepy, don't you think?

"It sounds like the rule of nations out there in the real world. It's either sad or scary."

"It's both. In fact the slogan is a good description of how my dad operates."

"He must be a living nightmare. You know, this reception room is sort of uncomfortable. I had visualized sitting down at a private table with a double espresso, and maybe doing a little writing."

"You didn't tell me that you wanted to write. Ask the receptionist for a piece of paper and a pencil."

"No, that's alright. To tell the truth, I'm afraid our turn will come up to see the Practitioner and I'm not really sure I want to go in there."

"No sweat. I always just duck out. I'll just ask the receptionist where the bathroom is, and then we'll skidattle."

Sure enough, the receptionist directs us to a restroom down the hall (we already knew that). Out in the corridor we start walking and talking without any destination in mind.

"Do you ever put any of your writing on a computer?"

"Sure, I use a word processor at home. Do you have a computer?

"Nah, not at home. Dad (my spectacular, glorious, sick and twisted dad) won't let us own anything expensive. 'Go buy it yourself, if you want it so bad.' That's what he always says. But my friend Shucky has a computer and lots of cool video games. He loves this game called *The Defiers of Dogma.* You get to pick whether you want to be a Pagan or a Muslim or a Jew or a Well-to-Do Atheist. Then you join your own kind and have to face the Crusaders. The Pagans have a lot of magic and curses and spells, but the Crusaders, who are supposedly devout Christian, are ruthless and blood thirsty for their next victorious massacre. Well-to-Do Atheists have a lot of espionage-type gismos, but a mercenary can hire out for any army. A religious mercenary in the Well-to-Do Atheist Army can turn quickly into a traitor or a spy. The Atheist's gismos are far more advanced than any of the Medieval Crusaders' weapons, but the Crusaders outnumber the Atheists, so you never know who will win out. The Jewish pray in their synagogues and then they keep getting kicked out of their country, so the Crusaders have a hard time hunting them down. The Muslims are pretty evenly matched with the crusaders and they fight each other with swords, but if you get enough points you can advance to the future and the Muslims have grenades and homemade bombs, which really puts them at an advantage, but you still have to beware of spies and mercenaries in your own army."

"That's your friend's favorite game? What about yours?" I inquire.

"I like *Fierce Fantasies II,*" the boy's expression exudes enthusiasm. "At first it seems like a game of brains versus brawn. There is a nerdy guy with coke bottle eyeglasses and suspenders to hold up his oversized pressed pants. His name is Professor Bloomfield. His opponent, Zargoth, parades around in a little stainless steel bikini with a steel fig leaf and slippers shaped like gondolas with little silver wings on his heels. Zargoth has bulging veins in his neck and he looks so muscle-bound that his ferocious looking little head looks about the size of a peanut. Zargoth reacts to every situation exactly like a junk yard dog would. He growls and grunts, and then with a loud roar he demolishes everything in his immediate surroundings. Professor Bloomfield is a complete wimp. His mouth falls wide open, his hands start trembling, and then he usually trips on something and falls down. He'll lie on the floor with stars and birds circling his head, until a light bulb appears above his goofy face. Professor Bloomfield gets really great ideas, usually complex and sophisticated solutions that throw Zargoth for a complete loop, because Zargoth can't put two and two together for the life of him. Professor Bloomfield has access to lasers, and remote controls and X-ray vision, but best of all, he has access to molecular restructuring. The Professor is fairly skilled at burning circular holes with his laser gun, or activating escape hatches and vault doors with his hand-held remote control. If you click the joy-stick three times, but not too fast or too slow, the Professor's thick lenses turn glowing green and he can see through walls and trees and people or monsters. You never know what might be hiding behind a monster or a person, so the X-ray vision comes in handy. The molecular restructuring device has great potential, but Professor Bloomfield is always turning out unpleasant surprises. Actually, most of the molecular restructuring turns out pretty hilarious, even if it turns against Professor Bloomfield, and he ends up loosing the battle to Zargoth. Once he turned Zargoth into a fem-fatale scientist who outwitted the Professor using the Professor's own devises. She used his X-ray glasses to check out his red and white striped boxer shorts and stork legs. Next thing you know, she turned him into a kitten and took him home as a house pet. Once, Professor Bloomfield restructured Zargoth's fortress into a supermarket shopping cart. Zargoth is so big he was trapped like a crushed madman, his face beet red with anger. When Zargoth started growling and roaring, the Professor stuffed a transformer into Zargoth's mouth and tied a bonnet on the brute's head. Another time, the molecular restructuring device altered the whole planet into oozing globules of blubber suspended in a planetary nebula. The Professor turned into plankton (still wearing thick glasses) and Zargoth turned into an amoeba (bulging and almost busting out of steel panties). The Zargoth Amoeba managed to display a few anger issues, but he was pretty harmless without arms. As it turned out, Professor Plankton ended up infecting Zargoth Amoeba with a deadly virus. So basically, *Fierce Fantasy II* can get really unpredictable. I think that's one of my favorite reasons for liking it so much."

"What a trip," I acknowledge.

"Yeah. What kind of games do you like to play on your computer?"

"Actually, I like to write my own stories. Believe me, the stories are nothing like the games you just described."

NAPTIME

We head for the purple door, knowing that it enters upon the revolving floor, with its central purple bed, circling in opposition. Beneath the amber, pink dome of sunset / sunrise, we decide to rest our bones. I am more in need of a break than the wiz kid, but he concedes tactfully that he doesn't mind *kicking back*. He insists that I take the bed, and once again he props his head on his skateboard, revolving around me like a moon. I want to believe that the kid is considering my welfare first. It occurs to me, however, that his motivation may be selfish after all. He may have sworn off using the bed altogether after his Goddess Insect nightmare. I can't say that I blame him for his offer.

Briefly, to unwind, I watch the drifting clouds of the dome above. A heavy, dozing-off sensation comes quickly, and I am dormant within minutes of lying down.

The instructor is a woman, either of Chinese or South American Native decent. Her hair has grayed slightly from its original blackness. She wears straight bangs, encased within a straight edged cut that traces the firm line of her jaw, converging at the nape. Her nose forms a graceful beak, her eyes are lucid green. She wears a simple, but modern brown dress with a gold sheen to it. This instructor looks both kind and generous, yet at the same time serious and capable of defending herself forcefully.

Three other students join me. The instructor leads us into an adobe cave. The outside may be adobe, but the inside is wet, dripping and muddy. She demonstrates how the cave's mud is a perfect consistency for molding any number of three dimensional shapes. I feel excited to be part of such a sophisticated and multicultural sculpting class. (My only previous sculpting experience was in kindergarten, using colorful strips of Play Dough.) The instructor fashions two thin angular arms upon a funneling torso, and adds a dish-shaped head with a pious expression (created by two flaps of clay that form eyelids and a half-moon pancake suggesting a gentle smile). We students, are eager to submerge our hands in the muddy wall, to commence with the manipulation of our own masterpieces. I relocated my workspace a little deeper into the cave. The floor gradually slopes downhill.

I have barely abstracted handfuls of mud from the walls, when mud-caked bodies emerge from the floor and the deeper obscurity of the wet cave. I perceive that living statues are forming themselves, literal expressions of art that takes on a life of its own. This thought barely has time to register. These bodies are disturbingly deformed. They lacked any redeemable value as works of art, unless one is drawn distastefully to the macabre. These pitiful bodies lacked heads, and only a few have even stubs for arms. Worse than the headless ones, are the desperate sounding ones, with only the lower half of a head. These unfortunate creatures lumber up from the mud with gaping mouths for groaning,

As if a river had filled the catacombs of human remains, buried after a violent slaughter, the bodies, now after endless captivity, rise up with insatiable desire. Desire for what? Is it hunger, or a soulful aching for their restored lives and lost habits? These thoughts are depraved enough, but my fear is heightened by the thought that these bodies seek sexual release, hips shoving forward and back, in a hopeless dance for stolen passion. I am the nearest living creature within their armless reach. I feel a deep sorrow for their hopelessness, but my horror overshadows the morbid sympathy.

My sculpting class gone amuck, I resort to yelling, "Make it stop. Make it stop. Make it stop." It seems as if my voice, obliterated or muted, has sunk in the mud. But I force my lungs and vocal chords, "Make it stop. Make it stop!" A choked scream emerges.

As if surfacing from a long underwater swim, I gasp as a skateboard nudges me in the arm. The teenager is talking to me, "Wake up, dude. You're having a bad one, dude, wake up."

I feel disoriented and drowsy. The teenager encourages me to get up and out of the merry-go-round bedroom. As we step into the corridor, the white door across from us opens and a young lady steps out into the hallway. This young lady could easily pass for the daughter of my native South American sculpting instructor, from the nightmare I had just awoken. The girl is perhaps sixteen or seventeen. Her long black hair hangs behind her in two long braids, forming two coils of gleaming black along the top of her head. She neither smiles nor frowns, but remains neutral, her dark green eyes fixed, without emotion on our faces. She wears two dangling fish-shaped earrings made of ivory. Her necklace is also polished ivory. The necklace, in particular, gives her a savage, native magnetism. The necklace is ornamented with a depiction of a fan of bear claws alternating with talons from a bird of prey. She wears a one piece indigo dress, of a stretch material that reveals her fullness of figure. Except for a silver ring on one toe, her feet are bare.

"Hello!" the teenager's tone hints of a girl-watcher's whistle. "My name is Eric." He beams a radiant smile and extends his hand.

"Hello," her mouth curls gently to an elusive smile, and she offers a calm hand to Eric.

"Hello, my name is Jacob," and I too shake her graceful hand.

"My name is Zorra."

One beautiful woman appears, and instantly, our names are out on the table.

"Been here long, Zorra?" the teenager takes the lead.

"Seems like forever," she responds.

"I know what you mean," sympathizes the wiz kid. "I never did open the white door you just stepped out of. What's behind it, if you don't mind my asking?"

Zorra smiles at Eric's fumbling attempt at manners. "There is a swimming pool. It's quite unusual, would you like to see?"

"Only if *you* show me," the wise guy is weaseling his way, seeking her approval.

"Well, maybe your friend Jacob would like to see also," she turns her gaze to me.

"Sure, I'd love to see it, but you were just exiting, weren't you?" I like to respect a person's agenda.

"Exiting, entering, it all gets mixed up - here in this bizarre place," and she turns to reopen the white door.

Beneath the swerve of the opening white door is a parquet floor of arabesque tiles in black and gold and white. There is an M.C. Escher optical deceptiveness to the floor design, as if the white tiles float above a black pit. If I focus, instead, on the black tiles, the white descends to a sublevel. Set within arched alcoves, there are gold, chalice-shaped pots brimming over with palmettos and dwarfed palmyras. The walls are embossed with radiating clusters of anthemions, and striped, above and below, with Greek palmettes. There are curvaceous French settees with bird-claw feet and leopard-skin upholsteries. Massive, gold-framed, elliptical mirrors hang between the arched alcoves, adding to the spaciousness of the copious hothouse. Webbed glimmers of refracted silver light waver on the walls and glimmer on the Olympian copper bowls than dangle above, suspended from black chains. Blossoming vines and feathering ferns emerge from the massive copper bowls, reaching for the pool below.

Our escort, Zorra, is a vision of bold contrast to the radiance of the pool room. Her bare, milk chocolate toned feet against the arabesque parquet, and her hourglass shape in a penetrating shade of indigo, dark and mysterious against the shimmer and glitz of the bathhouse. Her gleaming black braids only add to the polarity. Her sylphlike movements, however, conform to the outlandish and lavish décor. I have seen this poolroom style somewhere, an Orientalism made popular in Paris and brought to silent films of the nineteen twenties.

"If you would care for a dip in the pool, there are rooms for changing around this wall." Zorra extends a *Vana White* arm, directing us to a gap in the corner of the pool room. (I'm hoping, for the sake of my olfactory well being, that the brainchild will take her up on this offer.)

"I don't have swimming trunks to change into," Eric protests.

"There is an array of freshly laundered swimwear in the dressing room," replies Zorra.

"Will you join me for a swim?" Eric asks Zorra.

"Thank you, but I've only just dried after a short swim, but I'll sit on the davenport and watch." Zorra smiles at Eric, then at me.

"Come on Eric, I'm sure that Zorra would guard our clothes." I suggest.

"You change first," the wiz kid orders me. I realize that this gives him some time alone with Zorra.

"O.K."

Behind the wall is a row of dressing closets. Each closet door is constructed of two square doors, a lower and an upper half. From the outside, the doorknob on the lower square opens both squares. After entering and closing the door, I notice a latch on the top square, for opening the top half like a window. I feel as though I'm in an old movie.

Across from the closets there are cubby holes of folded swimwear. I step back out to select a pair of swimming trunks. I find the swim wear comical and old fashioned. The men's suits have broad cross-stripes. They look like long underwear, slightly altered - one piece suits with a tank top and knee length shorts. The embarrassing part is the flap in back that folds down if unbuttoned. I have the option of blue stripes on white, or red stripes on white. I choose the blue stripes in an outfit my size, fold my clothes, and put my socks inside my dress shoes. I place my shoes on top of the folded clothes, step around the divider, and return to Eric and Zorra.

Zorra giggles and Eric laughs like a donkey. I'm hoping the suit is more comical than the sight of my exposed arms and legs. I set my clothes beside Zorra, who is sitting on the leopard skin couch. Eric stands on his skateboard, with his back to the pool.

"I'm not wearing a goofy swimsuit like that!" Eric declares.

"Well, it's either the blue stripes or the red, unless you want to try on a dainty little woman's dress with bloomers." I point out.

"I don't think so. I think I'll skip the swimming and join Zorra on the settee." Eric decides.

"Oh, come on, I'm sure you'll look quite handsome in the red stripes." Zorra wheedles.

"If you really think so, I'll give it a try."

Eric gives a push of his skateboard, and wheels around the corner to change. I sit down cross legged on the tiles facing Zorra. I can't really blame the wiz kid for getting all excited. Zorra looks stunning on the leopard-skin settee, her legs tucked up beside her like a Gauguin painting, (or one he should have painted). We sit silently, tongue-tied and self-conscious for a few minutes.

"You resemble someone who appeared to me in a dream," I offer for an ice breaker.

"I do?" Zorra looks up from her fingernails.

"I had a dream about an art instructor in a cave who could have passed for your mother."

"Was she a painter?" she looks directly at me, her jade eyes beaming with light.

"She was teaching sculpting."

"I have a sister in Uruguay who has a talent for sculpting."

"Are you from Uruguay?"

"No, my sister married a professor from Uruguay and moved there. I'm from Colombia, originally."

Eric comes rolling around the corner on his skateboard with his clothes tied into a bundle, the shirtsleeves tied into a knot. He's wearing the red stripes version of my turn-of-the-century swimsuit. With his long hair and goatee, he looks like he could pass for a gold miner living at the birth of the industrial age.

"You look dashing, just as I suspected you would," remarks Zorra.

Eric flashes his most charming smile, rolling up to the couch to drop off his wad of clothes. He steps off the skateboard and balances it, wheels facing up, on top of the bundle. We turn to face the pool. A slight mist rises above it. The corners of the pool are shaped like scallops and there is a golden honeycomb trim that surrounds the edge. In the center of the pool is a small geyser of bubbling water. Eric turns to Zorra, "Keep an eye on my wheels, would you?"

"Certainly," states Zorra, in a matter-of-fact tone, she sounds obedient.

Eric takes off running and leaps into the air, grabbing his knees, to make an impressive water bomb. The splash of water soaks me, but the coolness of it is inviting compared to the tropical humidity of the steamy room. I'm not as much the dare devil as Eric, so I walk to the pools edge to gage the depth of the water. I also look for the underwater structure that is gushing the fountain of water in the center.

"The water is very deep. You won't hit the bottom," Zorra informs me as if reading my mind.

Nonetheless, I spot some steps entering the bright water beside the scallop shaped corner. "What happened to Eric? I would have expected him to surface by now." I wonder.

"I'm sure he's fine. There's a pleasant surprise beneath the surface," Zorra warns me.

"What kind of surprise?" I look back at her suspiciously.

"I don't want to spoil it for you. You'll be delighted, I'm sure," she assures me.

....

I push off of the underwater steps, and submerge into the blissful coolness of liquid. I open my eyes beneath the surface, hoping to spot Eric holding his breath, maybe sneaking up to surprise me. Eric is nowhere in sight, but below me is a motion of brown and green, a swaying motion. I resurface for air and then dive deeper, hoping to make out the blurry movement below me. I have a strong frog kick for a swimmer. I notice that my hands are as white as the door we opened to enter the swimming pool. Even with my fingers spread, my hands look like fists before me. I suspect that the pool lighting has created this effect, and then I clearly see that my hands are paws and my arms have white fur. I turn my head to look at my legs, and I see a long white tail behind me. I am a white cat! "Cats don't like water," I think, preparing to panic, but *breaking the rules of logic* has become the rule around here, and I have to admit that, as a cat, I am quite pleased to be swimming. In fact, I don't even seem to be holding my breath. My lungs are as happy as fish lungs, but I am a white cat, diving down to discover that the brown and green blur of motion is the lilting seaweed that I have gazed upon through the hallway floor in this place. Ahead of me, a beam of light radiates from above. I swim in that direction. As I drift up toward the beam, I see a square of light above, like a table top of light. I drift upward a bit more, and I can make out a child kneeling down on a sheet of clear glass. It is the little girl I met on the playground, the same girl I encountered again on the sailboat - the little girl who appears in my glass marble. She is smiling and waving at me. With every intention of waving back, I discover that as a swimming cat, I am unable to wave. I circle around below her, rolling and frolicking like a dolphin. I want to acknowledge her, and the word *hello* comes out of my mouth as **Meow.** "Meow," I say again and she waves to me once more. I roll over and below me, above the swaying seaweed, a gigantic dragonfly crosses the tops of the seaweed. This dragonfly flaps its large wings gently, and slowly, as a stingray would swim along the ocean floor. If this had been a dream, such a large dragonfly would terrify me. As it is, the absurdity of its size, and the sight of a dragonfly swimming underwater - these oddities are enchanting combined with the iridescence of its metallic green, purple sheen, and shining blue-black body. Fear does not register as a reaction.

The little girl stands up and walks off the glass square. I realize that she is in the corridor of colored doors. I swim further away from Zorra in the poolroom, and beyond the beam of light from the view-window in the hallway floor. I approach a green, rough, jagged wall. The wall slopes at a gradual incline. The stone wall is speckled with tiny silver mica freckles, and the motion of the water makes the sparkling mica appear like fairy dust in the water. I swim upward along the green wall. I wish I had a souvenir photo of this – a big white cat swimming up in fairy dust along a green stone cliff. "And here I am in the pool on my vacation" would be written on the back of the photo.

The water surface above me comes into focus and I can see that the surf is splashing mildly against the green crag. As I surface, I spot a small ledge of white sand, only a short swim from the green obelisk that juts out of the spray of water. I crawl up onto the sand and look, awestruck at the sight of the green, polished-rock tower nearby. Up at a height I would refuse to climb up on a ladder, I see small square openings, windows or eyeholes, I'm not certain what. My attention shifts to the latest transition in myself. I am no longer a white cat, just a white man in a goofy blue striped swimsuit.

I dive back into the water, anxious to re-experience the elation of a cat that can swim. Sure enough, I'm white and furry again, and my long tail sways and curls behind me. I swim back to the square glass that separates the water from the hallway floor above. I don't see anybody upon the glass, but at close inspection I can see the girl's handprints. She may not be a real girl, but I miss her. She seems like a sweet child.

I continue in the direction of the swimming pool, which I recognize when I spot the geyser of bubbling water that ascends from the seaweed like a thick rope. Surface into the hothouse, I find Eric sitting on the tiles, dripping wet, his hair slicked back. He leans back slightly, propping himself on his elbows, his ankles crossed.

"She's gone. She ditched us," he claims with disappointment.

I raise myself up on the underwater steps and spot the leopard-skin couch. "She left our clothes," I point out, fishing for a cheerful note.

"I would rather that my clothes walked off, and she stayed put," he declares dejectedly.

I pause in acknowledgement of his disappointment. "Well, that was like no swim I've ever taken. I turned into a white cat underwater and I found the glass floor that we've looked through in the hallway."

"That big white cat was you? I saw you! I saw you, man, and I didn't even know it was you. Hey, dude, you'll never guess what I turned into."

He smiles at me with that challenging look of his.

I look at him, from left eye to right eye, as if following a pendulum, wondering what he would turn into. "A dragonfly!" We both say in unison.

"I did see you, I just had no idea it was you. Hey, you might not be such a bad match for that Goddess Insect Lady after all."

"Very funny, dude. The Insect Lady is ancient history. The only girl for me is Zorra, but she gone and tricked us, and ditched us like two dumb suckers."

"Don't get so down about it. We'll probably see her again. I keep seeing that little girl that gave me the marble." Just then, I remember that I left the marble in my pants on the settee. I zip over to the leopard-skin couch and check my pants pocket for the glass marble. "Thank God, it's still there."

"Zorra doesn't look like the thief type," professes the wiz kid.

"Apparently not. I'm going to change back into my dry clothes. You're not going to disappear like Zorra, are you?"

"Nah, I'm not runnin' off anywhere. I have to change my clothes, too."

I go back to the changing closet. There's a metal hook, for hanging the wet suit. There's a dry towel folded on a shelf, so I dry myself off. By the time I dry myself off, get dressed, and round the corner, I hear Eric talking.

"We'll have to go swimming together next time, O.K?"

"I'd like that," says Zorra who has returned to the leopard-skin couch while I was dressing.

"Hey, we're glad to see you back." I tell her. "Where did you disappear to?"

"Oh, I just crossed the hallway to use the powder room. How was your swim?" she flashes an ear-to-ear smile and winks.

"Veeery interestink," I give it my best German accent.

DAY-GLO ORANGE

Eric leads us to a gaud-awful Day-Glo orange door. He has offered Zorra a lift on his skateboard. With curled fingertips, Eric pulls Zorra as if he were a beast of burden and she were the Queen of Sheba herself. It's another "Kodak moment" for my vacation scrapbook. On the back of this photo it will read, "*My tour guides*".

"The only color worse than this door is Day-Glo orange with dirt marks on it," I offer my aesthetic opinion. The saving grace is that the door is clean, but the hallway is dark polished mahogany, and the combination is sickening. "The worst of the sixties," I add with disgust.

Eric locates the correct key, swings open the door and bows deeply with one hand behind him, and with the other, a sweeping gesture of *entrée vu*. Zorra delicately dismounts the skateboard, and crosses the threshold like a cautious *Alice in Wonderland*, her palms forward, arms slightly back, just I would imagine Alice encountering a new wonder. The simple apartment is far less than impressive, but I stand gaping at a previously envisioned scene. "Déjà vu!" I exclaim with slight confusion. I then realize that upon entering my first door, the aqua door, I had expected to encounter this quaint setting. Surely the room is an old and worn studio apartment, and we will find the old spinster in the kitchen pouring a cup of hot tea. The antique furniture is all but smothered in doilies and quilts. Tiny porcelain figurines of Little Bo Peep and her flock accompany matching vases adorned with plastic roses of pink and white. Knitting needles and a ball of yarn rest domestically on a drab recliner that sags sadly in the seat cushion. There is an old Zenith television near the lacy-curtained window. The Zenith set seems to stare at us like a giant eye, but the screen is dark, greenish gray. It is obviously turned off. The T.V. stand is an ersatz wrought iron contraption with slanting shelves below for books and magazines. There rests a copy of *The Joy of Cooking* along with well kept issues of *Better Homes and Gardens* and *Sunset Magazine*. On top of the Zenith set is one of many doilies scattered throughout the room. This elaborate doily, spilling fringe over the top of the screen, protects the pinewood finish for the placement of a dual-antennae contraption. *Rabbit ears*, we called them, back in those antediluvian days. The rabbit ears are sufficiently padded with brown felt, but old ladies are known to have obsessed with the crocheting of doilies for all visible surfaces.

I had anticipated that Eric would locate the old gal and hit her up for some cookies and milk or some such granny delight, but instead he pulls the ON button of the Zenith set, selects a news channel, and crossing the room, flops down on the plastic-covered couch and pats the cushion beside him (as a signal for Zorra to join him). Zorra glances at me before complying, and I pick a chair opposite the recliner. My chair is also preserved in a thick plastic cover that squelches rudely as I wriggle into position.

"Who lives here?" I enquire.

"Beats me, they're never home," counters Eric.

The idea of watching the news strikes me as perplexing. Are we picking up a station from outside? Is this going to be the *real news*, catching us up on all we've missed while we've been trapped in here? Or is this some *dreamworld – fantasy news,* as unreliable as all the logic defying experiences we tend to encounter here? Within minutes, I have sided with the *dreamworld-fantasy-news* conjecture, but the report leaves me wondering, nonetheless.

"We bring you now to Denver, Colorado, where Mark Chenoval gives us live coverage of one of several alarming reports that we are receiving nationwide." *'Thank you, Shirley. I am standing on the capitol steps, outside the Capitol Building in Denver, Colorado, where Senator Allen McCormick has only minutes ago confirmed that Governor Wilson has declared a statewide emergency alert. This emergency alert, combined with similar reports in three other capital cities: Austin, Texas; Providence, Rhode Island; and Juneau, Alaska, has lead to hastening rumors that President Greenfield will be calling a prompt State of the Union Address concerning national security. We expect to hear word of this development within the hour. Apparently, according to Senator McCormick, the Air Force Academy, located in the foothills of the Rocky Mountains, about fifty miles south of Denver has been attacked, severely damaged and disabled. We have confirmation that military installations hidden underground have been disabled, if not entirely destroyed. Colorado Springs, a city very near the Air Force Academy, is currently being notified for emergency evacuation. As of yet, we have no information as to the nature of this attack, whether by bombing, or subversive insiders who could have turned hostile in other manners. Any number of possibilities remain, as yet, without verification, as we await further news on this truly horrifying development, here in Colorado, and likewise, as I have mentioned in Texas, Rhode Island, and Alaska."*

"We are asking all citizens and civilians to stay put if you are indoors. Please await further instructions and upcoming reports. If you are not indoors, if you are either traveling or are currently outdoors, please seek the nearest convenient shelter. Do not panic or attempt to interrupt public transportation or air travel. All ground and air conductors will be instructing passengers, and we are asked to follow these conductors instructions explicitly. Please do not attempt, I repeat, DO NOT attempt to leave places of business, shopping centers, restaurants, or any other public shelter. You are asked to remain calm, and remain indoors. Mark Chenovl, CBA News, Denver, Colorado."

"Thank you Mark, we are currently receiving live coverage of a dangerous and destructive situation that has developed in Juneau, Alaska. We take you now to Dan Quinsley at the alarming scene that is unfolding at this moment in Juneau."

There is a delay in transmission from Juneau, as we watch a bald man with puffy cheeks, who speaks without being heard. The picture flashes back to Shirley Thomas, who clarifies that there is a breakdown in audio transmission. "We take you to Maury Lezkovnik in Austin, Texas."

"*Thank you, Shirley. It is certainly chilling news that I relay to you, live from Austin, Texas. Approximately forty minutes ago, at 9:20 a.m., officials at the Capitol Building received an anonymous call, threatening the life of Governor Finchley, and warning that a bomb had been planted in the Governor's office, here at the Capitol Building. The building has been evacuated. Nobody has been injured here at the capitol, and no bomb has yet been found. Assemblyman Forsythe, had only moments ago reported that Governor Finchley was not in danger, that the governor was, in fact, on a leave of absence. Not ten minutes had passed since the report from Assemblyman Forsythe, when at approximately 9:36 a Forest Service Ranger calls in, reporting an explosion at Buchanan Dam. The disturbing reappearance of Assmblyman Forsythe, reporting from the Capitol that Governor Finchley makes frequent fishing trips to Lake Buchanan, and the governor's whereabouts remains unknown.*"

"Oh my God!" exclaims Zorra.

"This is cool," puts in Eric.

"I don't know whether to be alarmed or if I we should just consider this television transmission someone's hallucination, or a dream, or some virtual reality game like everything else in this place."

"I think it's real and the whole government is about to be overthrown," says Eric with glee. "Cool."

Zorra punches Eric in the arm. "How can you say that? People are about to get hurt, some people might already be hurt!" and she jumps up, crosses the room, and clicks the television OFF.

"Come on, maybe Jacob is right. We are all just dreaming this, so there's nothing to worry about." Eric crosses the room to click the T.V. back ON. "Besides, I was getting off on it."

"You're morbid," accuses Zorra as she picks up the knitting and sits back in the recliner, distancing herself from Eric.

The Zenith set is back on with live shots of a fire at the Capitol Building in Providence, Rhode Island. The reporter is reporting that an explosion of high magnitude has collapsed the whole east wing of the building, and emergency officials are concerned that the entire dome of the capitol could collapse in the resulting fire. We see the usual – bodies rushed out of the building on stretchers, and people running from the building, holding scarves, shirts, and jackets over their faces to filter the smoke filled air from their lungs. The reporter looks anxiously up toward his left. Gray smoke engulfs him as he talks. We have a brief shot of him coughing, and then he covers his face with his sleeve and the camera repositions to expose the burning wing of the capital, windows shattered and half the roof missing.

"I'm hungry," interrupts Eric, getting up and passing through the doorway to what is obviously a small kitchen. I can guess that the theme in there is chickens, eggs hatching, and roosters crowing at sunrise. I stay put in my plastic-covered easy chair. The Zenith set now displays a map of North America, with four pulsing orange starbursts: one starburst at the center for Denver, and the other three have been connected by straight yellow lines that form a lopsided triangle. The placement of attacks seems to form a pattern of center, northwest, south, and east. "Might we expect further attacks?" the announcer is now leading us all to wonder.

Eric reappears from the kitchen with a fluorescent pink plastic tumbler full of milk, and a plate stacked with *Wonder Bread* sandwiches. He offers us triangular sandwich halves. "What did you make?" Zorra raises her eyebrows.

"Peanut butter and jelly," Eric sets the milk down, takes her hand and leads her back to the couch.

The reporter from Juneau, Alaska is back on the screen, this time with audio. A map appears, showing Juneau along a finger of Alaska that hangs alongside British Columbia, far north of Seattle. There is a scattering of islands west of Juneau, in a pattern that looks like shards of pottery. The camera zooms in closer upon the map of Juneau itself, and we see an animation of a fishing boat with another pulsing orange starburst blinking at the front of the hull. Apparently, a fishing boat full of cod and mackerel, while passing under a bridge along the Gastineau Channel, had exploded, damaging the bridge and sending passenger vehicles flying into the air and into the channel. Shortly after the explosion, after tearing through the midsection of the bridge, the westernmost end of the bridge fell like a quick-drop drawbridge, and more cars slid into the channel. The reporter swings a wide arm upon the scene behind him, rescue crews with tow trucks, fire engines, ambulances, and a construction crane preparing to assist with the extraction of debris and sunken vehicles.

We seem so remotely removed from the simultaneous scenes of destruction, and yet I wonder if the overseer of this heavily guarded unamusement park might eventually deem it suitable to release us and evacuate this place for military or security reasons. On the other hand, we have all been told, by the news reporter, to remain indoors. The only remotely credible access to outdoors seems to be out the high windows of the shower room and out on the guarded sidewalk that the brainchild had described earlier. All the other simulations of outdoors, the playground, the tropical paradise beach, the sailboat on the ocean where I was given the glass marble, and the ominous jade obelisk at the far reaches of my cat swim; all of these strange and dreamlike locations seem more like tricks of the mind than the great outdoors. My poor, muddled brain is securely housed in this macabre funhouse.

How long have I been in here? A week? Four days? Or has time been flying by while I was having so much "fun"? Could ten days have passed? Is it the middle of the month? Has my roommate called the police and reported me missing? Will a snapshot of my face end up on a carton of milk or a flyer in the mail? And what about my job? Will they fire me? Have they already replaced me? Will my disappearance, along with Eric's and Zorra's become back-page news if our country faces large scale war, fought on our own soil? The Zenith television is just another funhouse invention. I have to believe this for now.

I have to. I would hate the thought that our life inside here became more desirable than life outside. It's all a trick. It has to be, I tell myself. I discover a lever near the floor, on the right hand side of my chair. It's a recliner chair! I'm wearing myself out with all these unanswerable questions. I close my eyes and the sound of the unfolding drama on the television becomes a far away jabbering, words tossed about like popcorn in a popper. I turn on my side so that I don't feel like I'm falling backward off a skyscraper. Ah, more comfortable. All feeling of sensation and consciousness leaks out of me like bathwater draining out of the tub. Like a needed release from sensory overload, I shut down, go blank, and fall into a deep sleep.

I feel my head bent up at the neck, and my leg bent down at the hip, as if I fell asleep on a collapsing folding-bed. I feel paralyzed as if I had taken an overdose of barbiturates (not that I've previously experienced this, but I can well imagine). I want to open my eyes or gasp for air, maybe just scream. I can't seem to open my mouth, let alone scream. There is a jolt of awareness. I'm in the old lady's living room with the Zenith set, and I startle awake as if snapped into consciousness by an electric shock. I prop myself up, half dead of exhaustion. I feel three hundred years old – fragile, weak, forgetful, and slow, (very slow). The Zenith set oversees the quiet room like a green-gray observer. The news has been switched off.

Zorra and Eric have left the room, probably for the kitchen and more snacks. I remember how much I used to be able to consume as a teenager – mounds of food like pyramids on plates, and then I could still go back for more. I shamble into the kitchen like a seasoned mental patient. No Zorra or Eric here, and I was wrong – the motif is not Cock-A-Doodle-Do or hens warming their nests. There are cat and dogs everywhere. A cat salt shaker and a dog pepper shaker. A *Felix the Cat* clock, hangs above the spice rack, with his syncopated shifting eyes and switching tail. There are kitten oven-mitts and cookie jars shaped like a Momma Cocker Spaniel and her pups. The refrigerator door is adorned with a whole kennel of cat and dog magnets.

Suddenly, to my horror, I realize where Zorra and Eric have gone. I feel like an unreliable babysitter, about to lose my job. I cross the living room, with a distinct feeling of being watched by the Zenith television, pass through a hallway, past a small bathroom, and sure enough, the door is closed. There is a macramé owl on the door. I'm not the babysitter, of course, so I don't barge in. I knock first. "Eric?" I call. "Zorra, are you in there?" No answer, but then I wouldn't answer either if I were quickly reaching for blankets or clothes. I open the door slowly. The bed is not made. There is a forest green knitted afghan along the foot of the bed, and the bed is nothing elaborate. Nonetheless, the bed frame is brass. Bob Dylan's voice pops into my head, singing, "Lay, lady, lay. Lay across a big brass bed". If the bed were made, I wouldn't bother to check the closet, but they're not in there, either (unless they can shrink to the size of mice and hide inside fluffy house slippers).

I return to the television room, feeling a little rejected and abandoned, when I find a note on the end table beside the recliner chair where I had slept:

> Jacob,
> Eric and I went down the hall to the right
> about ten doors down, across the hall. There is a
> see-through door that I want to show Eric. We'll be
> back soon, if you don't wake. If you wake up first,
> come join us there.
>
> ----- Zorra

I have no idea why I feel a sense of responsibility for the teenagers. I am not absolutely sure that they are both visitors from the outside world, but if they are – wouldn't a fifteen year old boy and a slightly older girl be in need of a chaperone? Without all the ordinary entrapments of parents and school and employment, not to mention all the possible consequences of unrestrained intimacy, the kids might end up in a sexual entanglement that could go sour or turn into an unplanned pregnancy. I don't think of Eric or Zorra as "uninformed" or "innocent," but the situation is abnormal. We are like shipwrecked survivors trapped on an island. What was the name of that movie that made Brook Shields famous? I never bothered to see it, but I suspect that the boy and girl characters had a few heated moments of passion on that island. I'm no stick-in-the-mud. I'd rather see two people make love than war, but I know a little bit about history, and there is no shortage of wars that were fought for the sake of love. The Trojan War lasted ten years, all because Helen was stolen from her husband by a younger man. (I wonder if Zorra is already engaged or married to some hot-headed Colombian.) We all know what a nightmare the jealous lover can be. Even mere lust can turn against you, leaving you with rotting skin, blisters, blindness, or a time-released inability to fight off infections of any sort.

I better go find them.

THE SEMI-TRANSLUCENT DOOR

The see-through door that Zorra had mentioned in her note is easy to locate. I wouldn't have called it "see-through" myself. The door is more like the frosted glass seashells that house the hallway lights. The seashell glass may appear amber, but I expect that the light bulbs give them the amber hue. This door has a misty silver-gray tint to it, and blurred colors from within the room cast smears of gold and white blobs that seem encased in the glass door. A white book, slightly larger than a paperback book, has been placed on the floor beneath the doorknob, wedged between the doorway and the door, leaving the door ajar. The teenagers have spared me from searching through my key ring. My fear of encountering careless hanky-panky now dissolves at the sight of this "open-house" gesture of the book wedged in the door.

I push open the door, and the white book topples over, revealing a title engraved in gold paint, **THE DIVINE.** Curious title, I think, considering that the book resembles a white bible. I pick up the white book, and enter the room, letting the door close behind me. This is not merely a room. It is, rather, more of an auditorium or cathedral. Long banners of scintillating cloth gently sway in an almost imperceptible flow of cool air. The banners are incredibly long, suspended perhaps from fishing lines that cross each other, forming spokes beneath an awe-inspiring dome. These gold and white banners are at least fifty yards long. If a helicopter were to rise up from the floor to the base of the dome, the height is perhaps fifteen stories.

The floor slopes gently toward a central opening, in a theater-in-the-round design. There is, in the circular pews, a reminiscence of the Coliseum, but the open arena here is much smaller. There stands, in the center-circular court, a tall gold obelisk. The obelisk structure resembles the jade obelisk that I had encountered at the far end of my cat swim. The gold structure is as tall as a lighthouse. In fact, there are rectangular recesses near the top that emit resplendent beams of white light. Some of the lower-level rays scatter and splinter throughout the gently swaying of gold and white banners. The mid-level spotlights form a starburst of radiance beneath the dome, and various upper-level rays fan upward into the dome, creating a dazzling illumination above. A thought crosses my mind, innocently, and with no intension of irreverence, but the whole cathedral floor resembles a roulette wheel.

"But where are Eric and Zorra?" I wonder.

I walk down the aisle about thirty rows, and turn left into a curved walkway that divides sections of the pews. I look down at the base of the gold obelisk, realizing that an entire football team could hide from my vision on the other side of the structure. I circle nearly a third of the rotunda before I'm convinced that the teenagers are not merely out of my line of sight. I feel inclined to yell out their names, but a sensation of reverence (due to the overwhelmingly obvious sanctity of the cathedral) leads me to shy away from disrespectful displays of any sort. I enter an aisle of pews, and sit for a moment with the white book, *THE DIVINE*, on my lap. A calmness and sensation of well-being engulf me. I feel consumed by bliss, until I realize that if Eric and Zorra had wedged the book in the door for themselves, I had better put it back. I'm halfway back to the translucent door when it occurs to me that they have a key to enter in the first place. If they misplace their keys, though, it might be a good thing that the book is still wedged in the doorway.

I continued back to the translucent door, and prop it open with the book, as I had found it. I turn and descend the sloping aisle to the giant obelisk structure in the center of the rotunda. Standing near it, I look up at the massive gold finger pointing up into the illuminated dome. Mentally, I take another snapshot, another one of my Kodak moments. The backside of this print reads, "Glory Hallelujah!" I have, in my life, come to believe in the practice of prayer, and yet I realize that I have not once said a prayer since I entered this weird "funhouse". This rotunda cathedral looks like a place designed for the purpose of prayer. I kneel down on the marble floor. The floor is cool to the touch of my fingertips. I put my hands in my lap and close my eyes. I intend to ask God to help us get out of here, but the first thought that comes to me is of Eric and Zorra, so I ask to not be separated from them. "Please, God, help me to find them, so that I'm not in here alone." An echoing chatter of voices from behind me cut short my requests. I turn my head, and at the top of the many rows of seats, the translucent door opens. Zorra , a tiny vision of black hair and indigo dress, steps in, followed by Eric in his white baseball cap. They're not loud, but I can hear the unintelligible reverberations of their voices. I stand up and wave my arms above my head. I can hear Eric say, "There he is, down there." He points down the aisle. They walk down the aisle as I walk up, until we meet about midway.

"I'm glad to see both of you," and I have to restrain myself from hugging them.

"We thought we'd let you get your beauty rest," Eric smiles.

"I hope it worked," I reply and now Zorra is smiling. She holds out her arms, palms facing up, and spins around slowly, "Isn't this place spectacular?" she half exclaims, half asks.

"Absolutely amazing."

"Have you had a chance to circle around the upper level?" she asks me.

"No. Actually, I was looking for the two of you, and ended up down in the center."

"There are numerous alcoves with a variety of fascinating displays," she waves a pointing hand along the nearest wall.

"It's better than any museum that I've ever been to," announces Eric.

"Let's show him the painted fish!" Zorra bobs up and down on her toes in excitement.

"*Vamanos,*" Eric chimes in.

We ascend the sloping aisle, the teenagers leading me. In one hand, Eric carries his skateboard like a schoolbook on his hip. His other hand rests on Zorra's shoulder, not with his arm around her, but gently on the shoulder nearest him. My parental alarms are lighting up like a switchboard, but I keep my mouth shut. A hand on a shoulder could mean nothing more than platonic friendship. At the translucent door, we turn left and soon we come upon the first alcove. Inside a mummy-sized recession, there is a colorful replica of the Tree of Life encased in a bell jar. Miniature oranges, apples, cherries, mangoes, guavas, and bananas ripen, decay and fall, all from the same tree. The tiny leaves turn brown and orange, golden and vermillion, and then fall in a ballet of fluttering butterflies. The ground darkens, and the tree stands barren, and snow gathers on the limbs and piles onto the ground until little sprouts peek up out of the shrinking snow. Tiny buds form on the limbs and then burst into newborn leaves, unfolding into an array of flowers adorning the tree like a full-spectrum bouquet. The flowers shrivel and present their fruits again, and the cycle of decaying and drying is met with a firestorm that engulfs the tree, leaving it charred black. There is a brief time of inaction, as if the tree were in mourning. Rich green grass soon carpets the ground at the tree's base followed by an extravaganza of wild flowers that blossom with a wild enthusiasm of violent and passionate colors. A downpour of drizzle fogs over the bell jar, and then the mist clears to reveal tiny new sprigs of branches that hold tiny new buds.

The exhibit appears to be a hologram in motion, strongly captivating the observer. Zorra tugs at my sleeve, "I want you to see the painted fish."

I follow the teenagers again. Eric has both arms up, balancing his skateboard on his head (at least he's not riding it in the sanctuary). We come upon another alcove with curved white steps inside. The steps are a bit large for ascending, but they are tiered perfectly for a small group of people to sit in a semi-circle. (Perhaps this is a storytelling room, I think.) Zorra sits down inside the alcove and I join her. Eric stands for a moment outside the alcove. He places his skateboard inside, near our feet, and sits down on the board, cross-legged. Behind Zorra's head, on a curved white shelf like the bench we are sitting on, is a display of wooden fish, painted vibrantly. Each fish has a delicate stand, like an inverted golf tee. Some of the slender stems are short and some long, resulting in fish at various heights. The fish are not all facing one direction, as you would find in a school of silvery sardines. Instead, each fish has his own independent direction. Although the display is motionless, a delightful chaos of motion is implied. The whole display takes up nearly the same amount of space as a large fishbowl.

Zorra begins to tell us a story, but I am entirely unable to follow it. I realize quickly, by the rough consonant-filled dialect, that she is speaking in a tongue native to South America. The vibrant display of fish is now swimming, skittering and dodging each other as if attempting to escape an invisible glass bowl. Zorra continues speaking and she lets her eyelids fall shut. I follow her example, having no way of understanding her words. With my eyes shut, there is a pleasant, but unusual feeling inside my skull as if my brain, in small pieces, is imitating the chaotic motion of the colorful fish. The sensation is as gentle as feathers dancing in my head, but the realization that my brain is scrambling is not a feeling that I trust. I feel a gasp of horror rise up from my lungs, ready to form a scream from my mouth, but I laugh instead. A soft, feathery, scrambled brain is a new sensation for me. I want to throw a switch and turn it off. I'm on the verge of yelling out, "Make it stop!"

Instead, I open my eyes and I am flying behind a speedboat on a curving river. Zorra is to my left, and Eric to my right. We are suspended from a hang glider tied to the speedboat below us. The river is lined with Scotch Pines and fir trees, and the water is deep, cool blue, bubbling up in a fanned wake from the boat that imitates the fan of the ropes that tie our wings to the speedboat. This is what it feels like to be a kite, and better yet to experience it with companions. We swerve with the bends of the river, and we yell and laugh and scream, "We're flying! We're flying!"

Later, behind another colored door, I would look back on the sanctuary experience, wishing I had opened the white book and read from the text of **THE DIVINE.** What was the theology, mythology, or history of this sanctuary or church? Was it a church, or was it a subconscious fantasy from some eccentric mind? *The Tree of Life* seemed traditional, a conventional symbol from my experience outside of this "funhouse". The scrambled brain, however, followed by a hang-glide flight along a river seemed overly playful or recreational to find in a formal place of worship. Why is that? Is reverence limited to a serious nature only? I had to admit, though, that the image of being pulled by a rope along the course of a river had symbolic implications that do lend themselves to the idea of God. The words "led in his path" come to mind. Also of interest is the concept of being led on a path with companions, rather than being led on a path alone.

I don't have any recollection of landing the hang glider. Shortly after yelling, "We're flying, we're flying!" we sit calmly again on the curved white steps. Eric sits cross-legged on his skateboard at our feet. Zorra points down at him, "You're bleeding!" Eric lifts his arms from his legs. Sure enough, his pant leg is torn at the knee, and his exposed knee is wet with blood. He takes off his flannel shirt, which he wears like a jacket over a white tank top. With the sleeve of his flannel shirt, he dabs at the knee. "It's just a scrape," he assures us. Zorra kneels beside him to make sure. She takes the flannel shirt from Eric, and gingerly dabs at his knee. "It looks like an open cut to me. It might need stitches."

"And where do you suggest I find a doctor? We're lost in La-La Land, remember?"
Eric stands up, "I'm O.K., nothing to worry about."

"What about the practitioner?" I point out.

Zorra, still kneeling, parts the tear in Eric pant knee. "There's a lot blood," and she ties the shirt around his knee. "You don't want it to get infected."

"O.K., let's get it over with," Eric complains with a smirk.

We exit the sanctuary, and Zorra is now pulling Eric, who rides the skateboard. As usual, the wheels create a racket on the wood floors. We locate the salmon door, and Eric has the key ready for Zorra. We enter the reception room, and the receptionist's mascara-painted eyes look up at us. Her rectangular reading glasses rest on the tip of her nose, below her eyes. Today her sculpted hairdo features the curled wave crashing the invisible shore above her head like a geriatric Mohawk. This looks slightly less ridiculous than her previous look with the wave over her ear. Her dress today is forest green, with a swooping collar that makes a chess pawn of her head. "Good Morning, how are you young folks this morning?" "O.K.," claims Eric. "Actually he's slightly injured," corrects Zorra, now positioned at the window facing the seated receptionist. "Oh dear!" exclaims the round faced woman. "Just a scratch," Eric downplays it. "The Practitioner has three clients ahead of you. Please, help yourselves to the refreshments," the receptionist tells us, like a trained parrot. She points to the end table beside the salmon couch, where a tired looking woman holds a small girl on her lap.

"His name is Eric," I add. The receptionist is writing numbers inside boxes on a stack of papers on her desk. "Oh, we know Eric well," she responds without looking up. I look at Eric and we exchange a puzzled look.

I set out to make my packaged cappuccino, and Eric has already located a copy of *Science Psyche,* and he places his skateboard beside Zorra's legs. Zorra has taken a chair by herself in the corner, so Eric lowers himself to a seated position beside her on the skateboard, with his injured leg straight out. As I stir the plastic spoon into the Styrofoam cup, I look around the room. There is a watercolor painting of an elderly woman sleeping on a park bench that I hadn't noticed before. Once again, I read the embroidered slogan from Orwell's *1984*. A disturbing feeling of confusion comes over me, and I walk over to Eric, whose nose is buried in the magazine. I tap him on the leg with my shoe, and point, furtively, to the embroidered slogan on the wall. Both Eric and Zorra look across the room to the quotation, WAR IS SLAVERY, FREEDOM IS STRENGTH, IGNORANCE IS PEACE. The words have been rearranged since our last visit, making the slogans misquotations from the original book. "Life as usual in here," says Eric with a shrug, and Zorra looks at me with such a blank face that I feel no need to explain.

A corner door opens, and a young girl, perhaps Zorra's age, stands in the doorway with a clipboard. "Dolores Manning?" she calls out. The tired looking woman with the small girl on her lap raises a hand before getting up and following the attendant out of the reception room. There is a middle-aged man, slightly stout and dressed in black. A black beret tilts rakishly on his head. Gray hair pokes out from beneath the beret. I would guess that the man is bald beneath his little hat. The man turns the page of his newspaper, shaking it with a whip-like motion before returning to his unobtrusive reading. An older woman with white hair wears a red dress with pearls and black shoes with slightly raised heels. With a pleased look on her face, she must be the kind of grandmother that keeps herself busy with the cookies, pies and housecleaning, but who knows, she may be a lady of leisure, with a maid and a cook at home. I wonder if the apartment with the Zenith television might be hers, but it seems like a violation to ask her, especially since we helped ourselves to the place without permission. She transfers herself from a single chair to the couch beside the refreshments, where she picks selects a *National Geographic*, and leafs slowly through the colorful pictures. I take her vacated chair. I notice across the room that Zorra is looking at a glass marble in her fingers. "Is that Eric's marble, or do you have your own?" I ask her, loudly enough for all to hear. Zorra looks up, but Eric answers for her, "She has her own. She calls it her *Wonder Book*."

"It's similar to reading a book, actually more like living a book," she comments.

"She instructed me to use mine like a transporter," Eric continues. "If I think about a place, a person, a feeling, or even a question, like: *'What is China like?'* the marble transports me into the spirit of a person in that place or circumstance."

"That's why it reminds me of reading books," Zorra adds.

"If I transport myself into a grocery bagger at a supermarket, and I get fed-up with the repetitiveness of the job, all I have to do is to wonder what the bagboy does when he gets off work, and I skip forward in time."

"Hey, a policeman could solve murders and other crimes easily with this!" I interject.

"That's a great idea, dude. The only thing I haven't figured out is if the people in the marble are real or made up or imaginary."

"They seem real enough to me," responds Zorra.

"A lot of things seem real here," points out Eric. The receptionist looks up from her desk, and Eric makes a sly expression, like a second grader getting caught shooting paper wads. I interpret his cue as an indication that our speculations about the marble might be misunderstood or used to our disadvantage, so we end the open discussion.

The corner door opens again, and a young man with slicked back hair and a tiny mustache is calling the name, "Jerome Harrington," and the stout man in the black beret follows him out of the room. Before the door closes, another man rolls out of the corner door in a wheelchair. This man is thin, and he wheels the chair manually across the reception room, toward the salmon entrance door. I get up, half of a cappuccino in one hand, and with my other hand open the door for him. "Thank you," he says without looking up. "Sure," I answer. The older woman with the white hair and red dress smiles at me, and I return a smile. I can tell that I like her, she seems very upbeat.

Now the tired looking lady with the small girl is coming out of the corner door, and the blond girl appears behind her to call out, "Edith Pixley?" The white haired woman carefully replaces the *National Geographic,* and she's saying, "That's me, honey. I may be slow, but here I come." A series of smiles are exchanged around the room and the white haired lady patters through the corner door.

I'm tempted to pull out my glass marble and try transporting myself elsewhere. Somehow, though, I don't feel like taking my first expedition in such a public place, so I reach for the *National Geographic.* From across the room, Zorra is giggling about something that is happening through her marble incarnation. Eric looks up from his *Science Psyche* to see if he should be getting jealous about her laughter. I'm looking at fishing boats in Canada and nomadic tribes in Mongolia. Now the corner door opens and the young man with the slicked back hair and a thin mustache calls out, "Jacob Lowe."

"Actually, it's Eric who is here to see the practitioner," I respond, standing up and pointing to Eric, seated on his skateboard.

"One moment," says the assistant with the small mustache. He walks over to a waist-high gate that accesses the receptionist's desk. The receptionist points to something on her desk. The young man picks up the folder and re-enters the room, "Eric Elliot?"

"That would be me, in all my glory," the wiz kid is hamming it up. Eric rolls over onto the floor and then maneuvers himself into a standing position without bending his cut knee. "Keep an eye on my board," he instructs Zorra, who places the skateboard on her lap.

The assistant the slicked back hair escorts Eric through a cantaloupe colored hallway with honeydew colored doors. The carpet is icy-blue gray, and the color combination is lighthearted. Eric anticipates a good feeling about this practitioner, based on the choice of colors. The honeydew-colored doors are not labeled with numbers or letters, so when the mustached man opens one, Eric is wondering how to tell which door is which. Stepping inside the room, there in the center, is a mat topped table, perhaps a massage table. The room has one window, with electric blue curtains, pulled wide to a view of lilacs, reminding Eric of the lilac blossoms outside the shower rooms.   Beyond the lilac bushes, a modern business complex with dark mirrored windows stands secure and uninviting.   There's a narrow filing cabinet in the corner of the room. A stylish, art nouveau lamp rests on top of the filing cabinet.   In another corner is a large, comfortable, stuffed chair. The same electric blue curtain fabric covers the chair.

"The Practitioner will be with you momentarily," informs the young man, who exits and closes the door with a click of the latch.

Eric moves to the window.   He can see the sidewalk below, two stories down, through the wrought iron bars protecting the window.   Don't nurses and assistants usually speak of a doctor by name – Dr. Langsley, Dr. Livingston, Dr. Kildaire, for example?   By calling this person The Practitioner, they have left him, or her, completely anonymous.   Here is one more quirk of this *Twilight Zone*, this house of multicolored doors. Eric sits in the huge chair and watches the lilacs, motionless as a still life out the window. There is a soft knocking on the door. A man with long, straight chestnut hair enters the room. The man appears to be about forty, forty-five, with a pony tail, a large nose (that makes him look like a seagull), and large brown eyes.   The man doesn't smile, and Eric wonders if the guy hates teenagers. The man crosses the room to shake hands with Eric, "So you are Eric, correct?"

"That be me," says Eric with a shrug.

"Please make yourself comfortable on the table. You may take off your shoes if you like."

"Are you the Practitioner?" asks Eric moving toward the table.

"That be me," says the man mimicking Eric's wording.

"Don't you have a name, Mr. Practitioner?"

"My name is irrelevant to my practice. Go ahead and lie on your back. Would you like a pillow?"

"Sure. Mr. Practitioner, I have a cut on my knee I want you to look at."

The Practitioner hands Eric an electric blue, horse-shoe shaped pillow. "Are you in pain?" enquires the Practitioner.

"Not really, but it's bleeding a lot." Eric unties the flannel shirt from his knee, and parts the torn fabric of his pant leg for the Practitioner to see.

"Looks like you took a bad fall. Let me grab some paper towels."

"Will I need stitches?" asks Eric.

"I don't perform surgery, but I do have a first aid kit. Pardon me one moment, will you, Eric?"

"Sure," responded Eric, lying back on the blue pillow while the Practitioner leaves the room. The ceiling is honeydew colored stucco. Patterns emerge from the ceiling: a bird with a long beak, a man wearing warped bifocals, a very hollow looking anguished face – like a Halloween mask.

The Practitioner re-enters the room with a white metal case and a stack of white paper towels. He opens the first aid kit, dabs the wound with iodine, and selects a bandage shaped like an X. "I have some interesting bandages in here. I think this one might hold the cut closed. I'm not a medical doctor, but I think you'll recover in no time."

Eric feels a wave of confusion. If this guy is not a medical doctor, then what is he, and why is Eric here? As his knee is getting bandaged in the bargain, he keeps these questions to himself for the moment.

"Good as new, just take it easy for a day or two, Eric. Shall we get started?"

"Get started? I thought we we're done. What is it you were planning on doing?" asks Eric.

"What we are going to do is entirely innocent and painless. It has been discovered that first-time patients have better results if they have no previous knowledge or judgments about the procedure. Put simply, you will be experiencing a sensation similar to hypnotism. More accurately, we will call it an experiment in consciousness."

"Oh great, it seems like I've been through a lot of those recently."

"Am I detecting a note of sarcasm or disdain, Eric?"

"Pretty much, I guess you could say that," says Eric, laying it on the line.

"Well, I appreciate your frankness. I would like to ask that we start today's exercise with a clean slate. We don't want to start off with any ill feelings, or bottled anxiety. It is best to relax, clear the mind, take a deep breath. Focus your attention on the moment."

"O.K. If you say so," says Eric with a tone of apprehension.

"I would like you to close your eyes and allow every muscle in your body to let go. Feel all the tensions drift away, out of your fingertips and toes, out of the top of your head. I want you to picture a chalkboard in your mind. With a damp cloth, I want you to wipe the chalkboard clean. I want your mind to be a blank slate. Relax. Breathe deeply. Breathe in once slowly. Hold the breath deep in your lungs. Imagine pulling the air all the way into your stomach. Now gently, let the breath out. Effortless, easily, slow your breathing and make each breath full and deep. If you feel sleepy, that's alright. Allow your body to go numb. Your mind is going blank. Continue breathing and I'm going to allow you a moment of silence to fall deeper into relaxation." (There is a pause that lasts about ninety seconds.)

When the Practitioner's voice returns it sounds softer. It sounds as if it is now inside Eric's head. "Eric, you're doing very well. Nice and relaxed, breathing slowly and deeply. You are drifting, you feel weightless. You are free from all concerns. You are carefree and relaxed, weightless and drifting. You can feel yourself lifting up slightly off of the table. Floating in the air. Drifting, ...weightless, ...carefree, ...relaxed. Continue to breathe slowly and deeply and you are rising up above the couch slowly, without effort without weight. Drifting, floating, relaxing, breathing, you continue to rise above the couch, up toward the ceiling. There is no hurry, just gradually, easily, drifting, carefree. You are higher up above the couch and you are getting near the ceiling. You are like a cloud. You are a puff of air. You are weightless and floating and gently rising. You are a gentle mist. You are happy to discover that you can drift right up through the ceiling and up through the roof. You are a cloud, an ascending mist of relaxation. Up… Up… Up you go above the roof up in the air, above the trees. Slowly, and gently, there is no hurry. There is no concern. You are carefree and floating. Blissful. Relaxed. Easy. Rising up and up, into the sky, drifting up into the clouds high above the building, high above the city. Happy. Relaxed. Carefree. Higher and higher. You are blissful and peaceful. I'm going to clap my hands now, and I want you to listen to my words, my instructions." (There is a slight pause followed by a slap sound.) "You are back on the ground, but you have entered a past life. What do you see?"

Without opening his eyes, Eric sees shaggy grass along a chain-link fence. He runs along the fence, low to the ground, and turns to retrace his steps, running along the same stretch of fence. A small animal in the yard next door runs through the yard, and Eric is yelling and jumping at the fence. His arms reach up at the fence. His arms are brown and black and shaggy. Dog legs. His voice is wordless, a barking sound. He barks and jumps at the fence.

"I am a dog," says Eric.

"Very good, Eric," replies the Practitioner.

During Eric's time with the Practitioner, Zorra's name is called in the reception room. Zorra Yoquigua is her full name. Full names link us to the outside world, to reality. Zorra Yoquigua has her South American background and heritage. Eric Elliot has his cruel and battered upbringing. Jacob Lowe, a truck driver for a mattress corporation, is trying to break into the world of writing, but remains an unknown author to the bustling publishers. Inside this labyrinth of colored doors and consciousness experiments, the three names are as real as Heckle, Jekyll, and Spreckle. And yes, I added a third crow into the cartoon, but isn't that fitting with the unpredictability of the Unamusement Park?

Somewhere out there in telephone books, we all have telephone numbers. We have addresses, and, except for Eric, we have social security numbers. I have not seen one telephone since my extended vacation in this loony bin. (On second thought, though, I wonder if there was an old rotary style phone in the old lady's apartment – on her bed stand, or on the lamp stand beside the plastic-covered couch facing the Zenith television. I didn't think to look for a phone or make a mental note of it.)

We're on our way to the banquet room for food. The Practitioner's office wore us all out, and we're getting a little cranky and need some nourishment. Eric is opening the gold door – he loves to be the keeper of the keys. He gives Zorra his customary Louis XIV bow in the doorway, with a grand sweep of his hand. Zorra and I cross the threshold like famished royalty. Eric and I take up our usual pattern of circling the table, snatching here and there at the deep, rich hues of gourmet food. Zorra stations herself at mid-table, daintily picking at blueberries, raspberries, and oyster-cracker hors d'oeuvres. She pours herself a goblet of wine so thick and dark, it looks like motor oil.

Eric has told us about his past life experience as a German shepherd. I laugh and poke fun at him, "Not a very high class background, dude."

"I love dogs," he defends himself. "I'm proud to think that I lived the life of a canine. In fact, the Practitioner asked me how I felt about it. I told him I was surprised, but that I loved dogs, so it didn't disturb me in the least. He told me that most people, upon discovering a past life as an animal, say almost exactly the same, 'Oh, I love horses,' or 'I love cats,' or even 'I am very fond of snakes.' Having lived a life as a specific species gives a person a special empathy for it."

I nod, and then I have a thought, "Why bother with the Practitioner when I have my own transporter marble? All I have to do is think, 'What was one of my past lives?' and the marble should transport me there, correct?"

"Actually, no," say Zorra. "The glass marble is capable of transporting me into the spirit of another person or animal. It doesn't work for transporting me into my own past or sending my own body to a new location. I have to leave my own identity behind. This change of identity is another aspect that reminds me of reading books."

"Oh well, I already have my own identity without the marble. I can't always remember…"

"I have an idea," interrupts Eric. "I might not be able to transport myself into my own past life, but I should be able to transport myself into Zorra's past, or your past?"

"Hey! I hadn't thought of that. They don't call you Wiz Kid for nothing," I smile and dip a chunk of turkey meat into a creamy mustard sauce.

"I'm not so sure I like that idea. It kind of sounds like *invasion of privacy* to me." Zorra points out defensively.

"Maybe you have <u>something to hide</u>," conjectures Eric, with a mocking, slyness in his tone.

"I have nothing to be ashamed of. I can own up to my mistakes. I can tell you, though, I think an author has an advantage over the reader – the author can leave out information of his choosing in his book. I don't know if the glass marble has the power to edit out parts of a spirit's experience without prompting from the owner."

Eric pulls his marble out of his pocket, "I'm beginning to like this clever little device more and more," and he shows off his pearly whites with a sinister smile.

"It works both ways, buddy boy," and Zorra gives Eric a huffy smirk and throws a cluster of grapes at Eric, which slaps against his ear. Eric looks awestruck. He glares at her briefly, dips his duck drumstick into a gravy boat, and sends it twirling Zorra's direction. She manages to duck in time, and the drumstick splatters into the lavish curtain, before sliding to the floor. Zorra stands back up, gravy splattered on her forehead, her indigo dress and her bare arm. "You're a pig!" she yells, and now she's chasing him around the table, without any luck at catching him. They run after each other, continually changing directions around the long table. Food flies in a variety of directions – puddings, pastries, and dark spews of wine from their mouths. Whole carcasses of cooked birds, fish and slabs of ham soar across the room like footballs. I duck under the table and let them have their messy little war. They're laughing and name calling, until Zorra is so out of breath see can barely cry out, huffing-and-puffing, "Enough, enough, let's call a truce." Eric tosses the soufflé straight up into the air, walks toward her, and then stops and bends forward, hands on knees, to catch his breath. "O.K., a truce," he looks up at her. They both have gooey smears of the exploded banquet in their hair, and their clothing is slimed and blotched of disgusting shades and substances that look like regurgitated garbage. A broken chunk of cherry pie slides from Zorra's head and lands on her shoulder. Eric is shaking his head and they both can't stop laughing. After a good two minutes the laughter subsides, and they're both using the ornate curtains to mop up their hair and faces.

I crawl out from under the table, "Is it safe to come out now?" I'm asking. Eric raises his eyebrows to Zorra, and they both scrape handfuls of sludge from their clothes to toss at me. I turn my back to them and cover my head with my arms. Zorra's shot falls short and splatters the floor. Eric's toss flies by my ear and back across the table. "No more," Eric cries out. "That's enough, let him be."

We decide it's time for a swim. "In fact," I suggest, "we might stop at the showers and spray off your clothes." They both agree, and we leave behind our world-record mess in the banquet room (for whoever it is who puts this nuthouse back together again).

A PROPHETIC DREAM

I've never had visionary dreams. The closest I've come to being an oracle is on the occasional early morning, when the thought of a friend I haven't seen for years comes to mind. Later that day we cross paths on the street. It's enough to make me wonder about cognitive thought, and the power of mind over matter. On one hand, I'm not inclined to believe that anyone can foretell the future, but on the other hand, I have very strong reason to believe that my entire belief system is limited pitifully to my own perception. Perception is so small in scope that I believe that any one person's world view is more a result of shutting out (or shutting down) sensations and input. A narrowed attention is paid to only a miniscule field of relationships in one's immediate surrounding. It is speculated that a person must protect himself from sensory overload, or information overkill. A thick nutshell of protection allows each of us the specialized freedom to focus without an endless array of distractions. It is baffling, perhaps even unimaginable, the number of *possible realities* that I casual discard daily with my narrow scope. I'm like a horse with so many blinders that I miss most of what is really going on.

As I mentioned, I've never had a prophetic dream before. If I did, however, I wouldn't have been capable of interpreting it. Today, now that I finally have one, here in this *House of Mind Games,* I begin to question the reality of my own self. If I fell into this screwball imaginary place, then what am I but a screwball, an imaginary person? I may very well be a screwball and imaginary, but I feel as real as I ever did. I take that for what it's worth.

Since the addition of Zorra to our little party of *tourists,* we have avoided the purple room altogether. I have sex-crazed, headless, armless, muddy ghouls awaiting me, and Eric has an overly lustful, overgrown Lady Goddess Insect, with a taste for ripping out genitals, awaiting him. Not only did we want to avoid springing these obscenities on Zorra, we also didn't feel optimistic about what might be awaiting her. We can always stretch out and relax in Paradise, but sand is not the best of beds, making its gritty way into undesirable body crevices and openings in our clothing. Worse yet, the sea always threatens to put on some kind of surreal sideshow. The old lady's apartment seems to be the best domain that we've stumbled upon for actually getting a decent night's (or day's) rest. (I never can be sure if it's lunchtime or midnight. Even the Felix the Cat Clock in the old lady's kitchen seems mysteriously unreliable.)

I make use of the old lady's bed only rarely. When I do, Zorra and Eric sleep on the couch, if they sleep at all. Usually, though, it's the other way around – I'm on the couch and the teenagers take the bed. Is Zorra already pregnant? Is Zorra even real? Lately, though, these questions have become the least of my concerns.

The prophetic nightmare came to me on the old lady's couch. First of all, the nightmare was merely that – a nightmare. I didn't know until later that the dream was visionary, that I would see the dream again when I was awake. The dream started with a trick of the unconscious mind, or of my dream-conscious mind. In the dream, I wake up on the couch in the old lady's apartment. There are white sheets covering everything: the Zenith television, the chairs, the lamps, even covering me on the couch. I wake up like a dead man, with a white sheet over my face. I pull the white sheet aside and get up. I go into the bathroom, where the sink and toilet are covered with white sheets. There are two white sheets covering the bathtub. O.K. This is not alarming. It looks as if a crew of painters may be on the way to paint the place. No problem. I go to the kitchen for a glass of water. Same thing. Everything is covered in white sheets. I drink a half-glass of water and wonder where Eric and Zorra have disappeared to. I cross the front room to the front door, and step out into the hallway. On every surface a white sheet is stapled – to the floor, the ceiling, and the walls. The frosted-glass seashell lights glow yellow-white through the sheets. The hallway is an odd sight, like being inside a white cotton caterpillar. Down near one end of the long tube, I can make out the tiny movements of people through a glass door. It must be the two teenagers, so I head in that direction. As the glass doorway enlarges with proximity, I can make out three figures, and I wonder who else is with them. As I walk even closer, shapes come more into focus. Not one of them is Eric or Zorra. Oh well, any human contact is better than being in here alone. From about ten doors down I realize that one of the shapes is the little girl that I met on the playground, the girl who appears in my marble. Beside her stands an old man with a long gray-white beard. In a chair opposite the old man, sits a disturbed looking woman. She is middle-aged, dressed in a white smock, with easy access, pull-on slippers on her motionless feet. Her head sags like a wet cloth against her chest, but her arms are feeling about, as if she is parting the hanging limbs of a weeping willow, or feeling her way through a dark forest.

I've arrived at the glass door and I wave at the sweet little girl. She waves at me with a timid smile. The seated woman, slouched and still flailing, opens one ominous eye and looks sideways at me like a lizard. She closes her eye and starts swaying in the chair, her hands searching the air frantically (for Lord-knows what). The old man looks at once cantankerous and congenial. Old-old men can pull off this look. This must be the old man that appears in Eric's marble. I realize, with a start, that I don't know who Zorra sees in her marble. Through the glass doors, behind the three figures opposite me, stretches a section of hallway that I have not yet explored. There are no sheets stapled to the walls and floor, but the décor of the hallway is much more modern than the hallway where I've wandered so far.

Abruptly, and giving me a scare, a Niagara Falls of water spills into the new hallway on the other side of the glass where the odd trio are stationed. Within fifteen seconds the water is up to the little girl's waist, and the old man's thighs. The disturbed woman in the chair makes no attempt at standing up or fighting the water. The little girl looks alarmed, and although I cannot hear her voice, she looks like she is yelling or pleading with me for help. The water rises so quickly that the old man and little girl are now treading water. The strange woman in the chair seems oblivious to the water. Her chair tilts back, and slowly rises in the water. I can see now that the woman in belted down onto her chair. She doesn't even open her eyes when her head goes under water and her hair fans out into stringy, waving tendons in the water. She continues feeling around with her hands, lost in some strange dimension of her own mind. Slowly, the tilted chair is rising up to the ceiling, where the little girl and old man look down at me, treading water.

I feel obligated to save the little girl's life, even if it means endangering my own. I pull on the handle of the glass door, and there is a squeak of rubber gasket. The door seems too heavy to pull, but I try again. It bursts open, knocking me back. A flood of water sweeps into the sheet covered hallway. I'm under water, swimming up to find the little girl.

Before I can reach her, I wake up on the couch in the old lady's apartment. I'm under a white sheet. I've returned to square one. I throw off the sheet, expecting to find sheets everywhere. It was only a dream, and there are no sheets draped over the furniture. I sit on the edge of the couch, elbows on my knees. I part my fingers like a large comb to run through my hair. My bladder is full, so I make my way to the bathroom. An ornately framed full-length mirror has torn itself from the large nails in the wall and has landed on a laundry basket, without breaking, in the tiny hallway to the bathroom. Was there an earthquake in the night? After relieving myself in a backed-up toilet, I notice that the sink and bathtub have backed up with murky, mucky water. The water looks like a pot of split pea soup has been tossed into it, along with tiny twigs and pieces of floating tomato skins and bits of soggy bread. The stench is nauseating. I head for the kitchen for a glass of water, and the kitchen sink has backed up with the same sludge. Fortunately, there is a cold glass bottle in the fridge with some icy water. When the question comes to mind, "Where are Eric and Zorra?" I remember the dream that I just woke from.

I step out into the hallway, and low and behold, the hallway is covered in white canvases that cover the floor, walls and ceiling. These canvases have been looped around the seashell light fixtures, so as not to darken the corridor. The appearance is not exactly like my dream, but it is close enough to give me goose bumps. Far down the hallway, where the white canvases end, there are people. This time I don't expect to find Zorra and Eric. I walk at a quick pace toward the people, and yes, there are three. Closer still, and I make out the little girl, the old man, and the seated woman. Once again, there is a glass wall with a glass door. The little girl is waving now, and I wave back. The glass door is open, so I walk right up to them and place my hand on the little girls head. She smiles up at me. The old man extends a mottled hand.

"Hello there, young man," his voice has a slight wobble.

"Pleased to meet you." As I shake his hand I'm thinking it's nice to be thought of as young.

"I see that you already know little Cynthia here," he looks down at the little girl. "As for "Sleeping Beauty" in the chair, I'm afraid she's wandered off to the far side of Never, Neverland. I'll introduce you at some other more coherent interlude. Her name is Mamie."

"My name is Jacob," and I offer him a trusting smile.

"A pleasure to meet you, Jacob. They used to call me Xavier. Now, it's mostly Old Man Xavier."

"Xavier," I repeat with a nod of my head. "I believe you know my friend Eric."

"The little whipper-snapper with his roller-skating surfboard contraption? I told him he was facing the wrong way when he put on his baseball cap." Old Man Xavier has a crooked walking stick that he likes the hit the floor with when he makes a joke or talks nonsense.

"That would be Eric." I admit with a chuckle. "He's a clever kid."

"Ah, heck, that kid's got a head full of words and not a lick of sense. I was just like him at that age. In fact, I'm still like that!" and he bounces the rubber padded end of his crooked stick on the floor again. He points his bent finger at me and adds, "Don't tell him I said so."

"Our little secret, Mr. Xavier."

"Ah, you might as well call me Old Man just like the rest of 'em," he assures me.

I just smile at him. The little girl has placed her hand in mine. I feel an inclination to tell Old Man Xavier about my visionary dream, but then I would sound like I was boasting about my fortunetelling abilities. That makes two secrets I decide to keep.

Eric would love to see Zorra with her clothes off. Zorra doesn't play hard to get. "Playing hard to get" involves playing a part, playing a role. Zorra may have learned to withhold information, but playing a role is not Zorra. Some would call this *deceit by omission,* but Zorra considers the practice of *the silent treatment* a necessary weapon and a logical defense tactic. Zorra owes nobody a seasonal pass, allowing complete access to her thoughts, opinions, memories, or even her past. There is a lead vault that closes as tight as a high-pressure, deep-sea observatory. Her sisters have used her words against her so frequently that Zorra has come to question the risk involved in being honest. Open-and-honest is a practice left behind as a toddler, left behind as decisively as crawling was left behind. And why wouldn't her sisters use information against her? They all grew up and learned from the Master of Revenge, their father.

Zorra's father is a hard-working man. He sells furniture and hand-woven carpets and bedspreads. He had a knack for buying and selling, and an eye for the unusual, but not so unusual that a piece of furniture would be awkward or distasteful. He knew what most people liked, what they had grown accustomed to, and he could glimpse the next turn of design trends, the next gentle step forward in a world of fashion. Not that he sold clothing or fashion, per say, but a truly modern and cosmopolitan home would surely compliment the fashion of its owners. "Is this such a difficult thing to envision?" he would repeat, day after day. And the Midas touch of all these talents was his ability to casually convince some unsuspecting browser, that this extra flair, this little touch of class, this pizzazz, was something that the homeowner needed and deserved. It was a form of flattery, a way of boosting these home decorators' egos. It was the recognition that this person was well poised, refined, a notch above the rest of them. (Little did this poised and refined Duke or Dutchess know that the next slovenly person in the door would also be well poised, refined, and truly a notch above the rest in the eyes of Zorra's father.) ***Frederico's Fine Furniture (Muebles Maravillosos)*** kept Frederico's family well fed, well dressed, and well supplied with the accoutrements of home and garden. There was nothing dishonest about striving for excellence, and striving for excellence was Frederico Yoquigua code of honor. Escaping the poverty of his own upbringing, Frederico considers his success a trademark of his own cleverness and endurance. Life is a struggle, the endless effort of fighting the flow of the river. The flow of the river is the nature of all things - to fall apart, to decay - to descend into chaos and poverty. It takes cleverness and endurance to fight this devouring flow of the river, to swim upstream is the task of a successful person – to conquer the odds, to reverse the pattern of nature.

Frederico learned early that people will envy your success and attempt to pull you down. Aimless drifters will try to take hold of your arms and legs and drag you down the drain. "You have to fight back," and Frederico raises a fist to the sky when he says this. "If somebody hurts me, I will hurt them back. And how could it be otherwise? Am I expected to stand here like a tree and let the offender come back at me with an ax until he has chopped me down to the ground? No, I must fight back. This is a law of success."

And so it goes. Frederico's little girls tell him all their dreams, all their heartfelt secrets. Early in their childhoods, words spill freely from childhood lips, and Frederico must warn his daughters when they are heading downstream, when they are giving up the fight to succeed. "Watch out for deceitful Prince Charmings, who will dazzle you with their smiles and their flattering words, but know nothing of hard work. They know nothing of the struggle. They know nothing of the war that one must wage to strive for excellence, to change a disintegrating world into something refined, something top-notch."

And so it came to pass that Zorra learned that to follow her heart was to cross her father's path. To cross Frederico's path was deserving of punishment, and Frederico disciplined his girls. Scrubbing, cleaning, cooking, mending – these were not punishments, these were the tasks of life to be taken head on. Punishment was exactly that, and it included a belt or a switch, and if need be, a sharp slap across the face. A slapped face was the remedy to foul words or disrespectful language. Zorra learned to bury her heart's desire deeper and deeper, out of reach from language and words. "Do not tell father what I am thinking or planning," she promised herself. Don't offer Frederico anything that assaults his own beliefs. It was Frederico's belief that everyone needed to learn - to think like Frederico, to pattern their behavior, and lives like Frederico. Not only did Frederico's family need to comply, so did the rest of the world.

It was no mystery to Zorra how her father could look at most of the world's people and call them hopeless. Most people didn't know Frederico's laws of success. Only a few, a chosen few had discovered these laws. Frederico would not stand by and watch his family live a life of ignorance and poverty. Zorra knew her fathers laws, and it took a heavy door to a lead vault that could withstand the severe pressure of the depths of the sea to lock his laws out.

Zorra sensed that there were other laws, other patterns, there were other realms of success. Zorra secretly tampered with a faith that saw no real need to swim upstream. In her mind's eye, in a place that dare not be spoken of, Zorra saw a river that flowed to the sea, and the sea was far richer, more refined, and far more than a notch-above anything that her father would ever imagine.

Eric sees all of this in his marble as Zorra lies sleeping beside him on Paradise's beach. He feels intrigued, even closer to her. He also feels guilty, dirty, and ashamed that he has spied into her life. He sees now, that if Zorra were to wake and discover where he had transported himself, she would snatch the glass marble from his hands and throw it far out to sea. She would scream at him, "Never, ever do that to me again!" and she would crawl off, crying. If he tried to touch her, to soothe her, to tell her he's sorry, she would scream, "Don't touch me!" He would know that he had wronged her.

He knows all this about Zorra because she is so much like him.

RENOVATION

The corridor beyond the white canvases is contemporary and spacious. Porous cement walls, ridged like accordion folds, loom twice the height of the previous hall. Narrow V-shaped light fixtures fan up from the floor at regular intervals. In the spear shape of these lofty stained glass lamps, I see the representation of falling stars, or paper airplanes descending. The tinted glass varies in design and coloring from one lamp to the next, and the mood of the corridor is altered by the hues cast upon corrugated cement. One lantern, like arms reaching for God, is cathedral-like with red, amber, white and blue tinted pieces, while another is calming with shades of azure, sky blue, pine green, aqua, and heliotrope. One lamp, like a premier-night spotlight, is silver-white and topaz. A vividly ominous mood is shed by a mixture of lapis lazuli, amethyst, and transparent obsidian. The wide floor and high ceiling are lacquered gypsum, exaggerating the sensation of expansiveness.

The doors, also, are taller and wider. I expect them to open onto conference rooms or courtrooms. These doors are painted in colors that test my ability to name: dried blood- red, magenta, ultramarine violet, grey-blue rain, powder blue, teal, ash blue, kelp green, military green, butterscotch, clay, mustard spice, brick, Indian red, tawny, earth, slate, chocolate, coral, apricot, larkspur, pewter, alabaster, lead.

Old Man Xavier has instructed me to follow him. He leads while Cynthia pushes Mimi's chair (I hadn't noticed the tiny wheels on the chair legs). I am taken to a door that I might best describe as faded avocado. The brass doorknob forms a sphere, and no key is required to open it. The huge door swings open and the four of us enter.

This room would make an excellent conference room. The sparkling ceiling is high like the hallway, and there is a thick, faux fur carpet of gray lavender. Tall grey curtains hang from the ceiling to the floor, and a dim light filters in through the massive curtains opposite the faded avocado door. A panorama shaped aquarium is built into the wall to the left, and at intervals a dense school of sardines overtakes the bright mango lit water with their metallic silvery sheen. On the muted lavender polar bear floor, forty or fifty chairs form a wide circle. The black chairs remind me of airport or planetarium seating: modern, cushioned and streamlined.

Old Man Xavier walks to the circle's center, turns and gestures that we are to join him by selecting a seat. Cynthia parks Mimi, asleep in her wooden wheelchair, between two chairs in the circle. She then crosses the circle to choose a chair for herself. Old Man Xavier takes a chair about midway between the two, and I choose a chair across from him. We face each other silently. I wonder, "What next, a business meeting?"

The silence lingers. There is a feeling that we are on break time. We look at each other and we look at our own hands. I look up at the weak light seeping into the room through the gray curtains. The repetitive passage of hundreds of glistening sardines adds a mesmerizing quality to our hushed composure. *Quiet Time.* I would rather be reclining on a bed or couch. I'm on the verge of a nap.

Earlier, I left Zorra and Eric back in Paradise. They were drying in the sun and I felt like a third wheel, the odd-man-out. I hope I haven't lost track of them. I wish we all had cell phones for checking on each other. I haven't tried transporting myself with my glass marble yet. Will Cynthia's face appear in the marble if she's here in the room with me? I hold the marble up to the light, and the pearlescent curls of smoke coil and swirl inside. The girl's face appears, but the expression doesn't match the "real" girl in the chair. I think, "What are Eric and Zorra doing now?" and the girl in the marble says, "One name at a time." I rephrase the question, "What is Eric doing now?" A scene develops in the glass marble. Either the marble is expanding or I am shrinking and I am drawn into the scene. From the perspective of my mind's eye, I disappear from the circle of chairs and leave behind the quiet-time circle behind the faded avocado door.

I'm in the swimming pool beneath the viewing glass in the old hallway. I don't see anybody standing on the viewing glass above me. The glass is not lit as usual, it is dark gray. The white canvas covering the hallway is dimming the light. I'm not a cat and I'm not swimming. I'm flying in the water – slowly, gracefully like a stingray. I am the giant dragonfly and it hits me (like a miraculous coincidence) that a dragonfly is so very much the spirit of Eric. It hits me deeper, and yet whimsically, that I am Eric. I turn a loop-to-loop with the thrill of teenage exuberance. Exertion feels so effortless.

A radiant and splendid sight appears before me, and I recognize the Snowy Owl that I had previously watched from the viewing glass in the floor. In the deep shining eyes of this remarkable bird I see a gentle acceptance of a passion that is all but bursting from my whole being. I am Eric the Giant Dragonfly, and I am madly in love with Zorra the Snowy Owl. We are both flying and swirling as if to a ballroom waltz.

"I would like to tell you a story." The voice of Old Man Xavier startles me from my transported state. I am seated in the circle of black chairs with Mimi to my left, Cynthia to my right, and Old Man Xavier directly across from me. I feel like a grade school kid caught reading a comic book, and I have to credit Zorra for comparing the glass marble to the experience of reading a book.

Xavier clears his throat and I place the marble back into my pocket. Xavier looks at each of us, holding us with his silence. Mimi still has her eyes closed inside her perpetually slumped over head. Her arms hang motionless over the arms of the wheelchair. Cynthia is sitting cross-legged, and with folded prayer hands she looks like the A student in the classroom. And who knows, maybe Old Man Xavier is a professor of sorts. He takes off his glasses, and gently cleans them with his shirt tail, clears his throat again, and begins his tale.

"I used to not have white hair. Nor did I have a long gray beard. I used to have a life awaiting me outside of this Land of Multicolored Doors. None of you were here yet, not even Mimi. Poor Mimi arrived a few years later.

She used to be more alert. She could carry on conversations back then. She was still walking then. She may have been a little skittish and overly nervous, but she didn't seem like the type of woman who would get lost inside her own mind. But like I said, she wasn't here yet. This room where we now sit wasn't here yet either.

I used to run a grocery store. It wasn't a supermarket, but it was a successful business. It was a neighborhood store, the type of place where I knew half the people that came in by name. I knew pregnant mothers, and then they'd show me their newborns, and the babies had rattles and bottles and stuffed animals. Before I knew it, the babies were seven or eight and riding bicycles or roller skates and rushing inside my store to buy candy and soda, or a bag of flour for Mom, or a quart of milk and cereal and toilet paper. There was a kind of magic about it, but you had to stick around long enough to see the magic unrolled itself, like a big movie up on a giant screen. If you didn't look for the magic, it was more like the same thing over and over, and it just wore you out.

One of the mothers who lived down the street came in one day to show me her new granddaughter. I remember that little granddaughter wrapped up in a yellow blanket and her bright orange hair in wisps around her tiny face. The proud grandmother, Jessica was her name, bought some oatmeal and bananas and a little jar of baby food (I think it was mashed yams or some odd food I'd never thought of babies eating). I gave Jessica her change. She stuffed the money into her brown purse, clipped the purse clasp shut, and then set her bag of food inside the baby buggy beside the baby girl in the yellow blanket. She was on her way out the door, when she squealed, "Oh, I almost forgot!"

She turned around and pulled a brown package out of her coat pocket. She handed me the brown package and I noticed scotch tape wrapped around it. "I have a present for you, Xavier. Here," and she placed the package in my hands, smiled, and then left.

I didn't even say, "Thank you," or "What is this?" or anything. It wasn't Christmas time, and it wasn't my birthday, and I didn't know what to think. A little boy with a crew-cut dumped some lollipops and Monster Cards with bubble gum on the counter. I set the brown package down and counted his dimes and pennies and told him what he had to put back and what he could purchase instead. After the kid left, the store was quiet, so I peeled the scotch tape off and unfolded the brown paper. It was a book. The title was *The Unamusement Park*. "Interesting title," I thought. I opened the book, and on the first blank page Jessica had handwritten a message to me."

> Xavier,
> My sister sent me this book a couple years ago, and I never have bothered to read it. I always see you reading unusual novels. Let me know if you like it or not,
>
> Jessica.

"I don't remember looking at the back of the book for reviews or praise. Did I look inside the cover sleeve for a short synopsis of the story? I don't think I did. Did I turn to the title page and look behind it for the copyright date? I don't remember doing that either. All I remember is the first sentence of the first paragraph of the first page: **"You shouldn't have come here."** I may be a fairly simple, law abiding man, but those words were egging-me-on to read a few more words. Before I know it, and you can't say I wasn't warned, I was lead into this darn hallway and the door was shut behind me and a creepy little guy is handing me a big ring of keys and talking all sorts of gibberish. The little guy disappears into his room before I can tell him that I have a business to take care of. I was not a happy camper, and I was not up for trying all those old skeleton keys in the locks of doors. The colors of the doors were like the carnival was in town.

After a few very unusual experiences behind door number one and then door number two, I started to worry. First, I thought I was dead, and this was my punishment, or this was my reward – depending on how you looked at it. How could I read a book that sucked me in so completely that I couldn't get back out? Something was going on that didn't meet the eye. I decided next that I was kidnapped, or abducted by aliens. Then I thought, maybe I've gone crazy. Maybe my brain just shorted out, once and for all. We see all those crazy people locked up in crazy houses. Some of them have to wear straight jackets and others have to be tied down, but we never see what's going on inside their heads, do we?

Then I decided that the government was using me as an experiment. That got me good and mad for a couple of days. It didn't get me out of here. Then I decided I was going to escape. That's a pretty good story I'll have to tell you someday, but you already know how it turned out, 'cause we're all still in here.

Time passed. Lots of time passed. This place gets a little scary and then it gets a little bit amazing, and it's not all bad. Just like our friend, Eric, I discovered that this place is well guarded. That made me feel trapped at first, and I wanted to find a way to trick the guards and break out of here. Over the years I've watched a few of those news programs that I know you've been catchin' on the old Zenith set in Rita's apartment. Rita is another story and she's not with us anymore. She died in her sleep, but she was such a sweet old gal. Nobody had the heart to clear out her belongings from her apartment.

Like I said, though, we've all seen the news on the old Zenith set. I used to want to get out of here. Now I've been in here so long it's become my home. The world out there with my grocery store and my neighborhood, I haven't seen it for a long time. There have been days when I watch the news and I have to ask myself, do I want to go back out there? Maybe these guards here are doing me a favor. You can argue with me, "Old Man Xavier, they've got you trapped in some guy's book," but if I get out, where will I be trapped then? In a grocery store? In a city? In a country?

Well, if they let me out of here, I will end up leaving, but not without trepidation. And there's always that place where Mimi went. Right Mimi?"

We look at Mimi slumped over in her chair, sitting motionless as a tomb.

"I could go on and on about my history in this odd place. The place has changed. It's bigger and some of the rooms have changed. There have been stretches of time when I thought that I was uncovering the nature of the business going on here. My mind has this unrelenting habit of trying to make order out of the chaos. No sooner do I start piecing a few bits of the puzzle together, and I am firmly reminded that the puzzle itself may be imaginary, dream-world, or illusion. I fall on my face or land on my head, and I return to the conclusion that my best bet is to not take things too serious. Probably more important, I learn to not take <u>myself</u> too serious. The funny part is that these are the same lessons I was learning out there in the "so called" real world.

But enough out of me. I have given you a bit of my own history, and now I would like to invite you all to do the same."

Cynthia and I look at each other, and then back at Old Man Xavier. Mimi is not very likely to jump in and tell us her life story. Cynthia speaks up, proving that she's not as introverted or shy as she may appear.

"I have been here a very long time, ...forever. I was only four years old when I first got here. I still miss my Momma. I used to cry when I went to sleep, but now I'm getting big and I don't cry so easy. At home I have a doll collection. I have about a hundred dolls. I have a great big doll house, too, but it's not for the dolls.

When I was four, after my birthday, we went camping in the backyard. It's not real camping because there are no bears, but we have a tent and we sleep outside so it's kind of like real camping. I invited Francis to stay overnight for pretend-camping in the backyard. There were lots of stars, and my brother Casey invited his best friend Dexter to go fake-camping with us. There were lots of stars and lots of crickets, and we had yogurt and trail mix so we could make believe that we were in the forest. Dexter wanted to tell us a scary story and Casey said, "Cool!" We all shined flashlights on our chins and pretended that we had a campfire. Momma said we weren't allowed to have a campfire without adults. Dexter wasn't shining his flashlight on his chin, though. He needed the flashlight to read the book that he brought. I think it was the same book that Old Man Xavier talks about. I remember Dexter saying that you better not go here, and you better go back. He even talked about Pandora's Box. I know about Pandora's Box from one of my fairytale books. Anyway, I was listening to Dexter tell the story and I liked the story because it sounded like something scary was going to happen. I was thinking about a bald man who opened the door and gave me a set of keys. He called them skeleton keys. I think they were for Halloween. I was listening to the story, at first, and I could hear Dexter's voice talking low and spooky-like. When he said there was a long hallway and doors in different colors I couldn't here his voice anymore, but I could see the doors because I could touch them and feel them. The story turned into my real life. This is my new real life, because I can't see Dexter or Casey or Francis or Momma or Daddy. Old Man Xavier says that someday I will see them again and all my dolls and my dollhouse and my cat Oscar.

I like to play on the playground and I like to paint pictures with real paint, not crayons. I'm going to be an artist when I grow up. If I live in France you can come and visit me. I like to ride in my Daddy's sailboat. Something funny happened. Daddy's sailboat is in my new real life, but not my Daddy. Old Man Xavier says, "Don't worry. Your Daddy is O.K." He probably sent the sailboat because he loves me and he knows I'm too little to swim in the ocean. I'm almost big enough to swim in the ocean, but I don't really want to anyway.

I get bad dreams and they come to get me sometimes when I'm awake. Some of the bad dreams are not so bad, some of my dreams are beautiful and I like it when they come and get me. Once I found a fluffy white bunny rabbit and I loved him so much that about a hundred white bunnies came to see me and I was still awake. Another time I found a cute little baby doll so I kept it, but she started saying bad words and doing bad things 'til one time she scared me so much that I threw her down in the wishing well. I'm afraid to make any more wishes because the drowned baby doll might talk back to me. Mimi is my friend, too. If you wait long enough, who knows, two or three days maybe, she will talk to you. I think Mimi saw some really bad things that scared her a lot. I don't blame her for playing Hide and Seek, because I might do the same thing if it happened to me. I'm glad that Jacob is here, too. He reminds me of my father except that he doesn't really look like him, not that much."

Cynthia folds her hands in her lap again and turns her head to face Old Man Xavier. It seems to be a signal that she is done telling about herself, which means that it's my turn. I take a deep breath and ponder where to start. The day I walked into the bookstore might be a good beginning.

Eric slips the glass marble into his pocket and looks at Zorra, supine on the sand, a large white towel wrapped around her and three other towels spread for the both of them to sunbathe. She looks serene and elegant, her bone earrings across her shining wet hair, and her savage necklace clutching at her collarbones. He knows that Jacob can be located with the help of the glass marble, and Jacob must have thought of this before slipping away, unannounced.

Eric lies back and closes his eyes. Zorra turns on her side, thinking that this handsome boy makes good companionship. She feels a love for Eric, as if he were her younger brother. She's not oblivious to his infatuation for her. She enjoys the attention, usually. Certainly if she were back in the world outside, she would brush-off Eric, knowing that an older man is a more appropriate companion. So what about Jacob? He's older, but more like her father's age. Jacob seems like a nice guy, although not exactly her type. He's more like the type that would make a good friend, someone to turn to share good news, bad news, or no news. He seems safe and comfortable, but not intriguing or aggressive enough to capture her sense of allure.

What then, succeeds to attract her? She is drawn to excitement, pizzazz, daring, and determination. Without having consciously conjured an exact label, what she wants is a warrior. She is too young to decipher or see in herself this ironic weakness – she is drawn to danger.

There is an imagined image that Zorra sees of Eric, a picture of what this boy might be like in ten or fifteen years. The image could be as much wishful thinking as it might be fantasy, but Zorra can picture an older Eric that she could feel a deeper intimacy for. But if Eric were older, Zorra would be older, too. And who really knows what the near future holds? What might happen in the passing of ten years? Eric could end up with an amputated leg, or turn into a criminal. He could come in contact with a fatal illness, or go mad. Eric could join the military and turn up lost in action.

For now, though, Eric is just a kid, a nice kid, a fun friend. It might look like they are boyfriend and girlfriend, but does it really matter here? Not really, she calculates. And who in this place is there to step in and take Eric's place? Nobody that she is aware of. She values the closeness and caring they share for each other. She feels less like a scared girl, falling into an unexplainable chasm of hallucinations. Comfort and security have resulted in sharing this mind twisting experience with another young person. Zorra is a good ally, but her wall stands strong around her.

Zorra gets up and shakes out the sand from one of the towels, then wraps her hair in the towel. She steps over to the clothing that hangs drying on nearby bush branches. Their clothing is only slightly damp now. She pulls her dress from the branches and returns to the towel beside Eric.

"Eric, your skin is burning in the sun here. We better leave."

Eric sits up and sees that his thighs are taking on a pinkish hue. He rouses clumsily, and collects his drying clothes. The socks are too wet to wear, so he tucks them into his back pockets, giving him the odd appearance of a rabbit with two sagging tails. They gather the towels. They feel inclined to clean up after themselves in Paradise, while in contrast, they left the banquet room trashed. Perhaps eating is not seen as sacred.

I'm barely piecing together my story, the train of events that led me to the bookstore where I discovered the odd book titled *The Unamusement Park,* when the faded avocado door opens. Zorra and Eric spill into the room of chairs in a circle. Zorra still has a towel wrapped around her head, and Eric has his ball cap on backwards, his skateboard in one hand, and towels draped over his other arm. I put my story on hold as we all turn in their direction (all except Mimi, of course, who remains a petrified rock).

Old Man Xavier is gesturing silence, with a finger to his lips, and with the other hand waves to the teenagers to come and join the circle. They select two seats together, midway between Xavier and Cynthia. Old Man Xavier points his long finger my direction, and I take a deep breath to resume my story. I barely open my mouth when a loud whoosh fills my left ear. A bright golden light bursts upon the circle. The whoosh sound reminds me of igniting a gas fueled fireplace. Hysterical screams from the girls, Zorra and Cynthia, fill the huge room. We all jump to our feet. Mimi's chair is on fire. Eric bolts across the circle and throws damp towels over the wheelchair, smothering the fire.

"Oh my God!" exclaims Eric, and we all gaze dumbfounded at Mimi's steaming chair, now draped in dirty white towels. The shape of the chair remains, but Mimi is gone. Eric slowly pulls the towels from the chair, and all that is left is the charred remains of the wooden wheelchair, and two smoldering shoes on the floor.

Zorra is dumbfounded by the dramatic disappearance of the woman who has guided her in her glass marble. Zorra had met Mimi in the hallway one day. She took pity on the poor broken woman, and wheeled Mimi to the banquet room. Mimi had refused the food that Zorra offered, so Zorra had packed a reasonable lunch for the poor woman, and then wheeled her to the Cathedral room, with its white covered Divine texts, and the gargantuan obelisk beneath the central dome. Zorra then wheeled Mimi down to the open floor that circled the obelisk, and there Zorra knelt to say a prayer for the poor, disabled woman. After the devotional visit to the cathedral, Zorra took Mimi to the Paradise beach. The wheels of the chair sank readily and deeply into the sand, disabling them from parking anywhere near the waves of the sea. The sound of seagulls and surf, however, seemed to stir Mimi to a state of communicativeness. "Florida, I'm home!" she said softly, and Zorra didn't bother to correct her. Zorra was able to feed Mimi a few bites of flatbread folded over ham, and a couple bites of a juicy plum that dribbled down Mimi's chin. Mimi chuckled. "Thank you, young lady," said Mimi in a hoarse voice. One eye parted slightly, a dead, dulled eye. Zorra concluded that Mimi must be blind.

Later, when Zorra felt exhausted, she brought Mimi to a dimly lit room that Eric and Jacob had failed to discover. It was a room with cushioned couches that faced a curtained screen. Zorra had discovered that theatrical presentations would begin if you pulled up the arm of the couch and pushed a green button on a built in remote-control. A red button shut down the presentation. With the remote left off, the room was a sound-proof, silent, and softly lit lounge. It served perfectly as a secure hide-away to stretch out and sleep. Zorra had once attempted to assist Mimi onto a couch so that the old gal could sleep lying down. Mimi stubbornly resisted all efforts to be extracted from the wheel chair, so, giving in, Zorra stretched out on a couch with Mimi parked beside her. No sooner had Zorra closed her eyes, when Mimi's low gravelly voice could be heard, "This is for you." Zorra opened her eyes to see Mimi reaching out. Zorra held out her hand and Mimi firmly placed the glass marble into her palm.

As time passed, Zorra had grown comfortable with the small face in her marble. The countenance of Mimi in the marble seemed more alert and capable of giving directions. There were days when Zorra felt confident that the engaging image in the marble was assurance enough that Mimi need not be checked upon. Mimi had gotten along without Zorra before they met, hadn't she? Zorra knew that this question was a rationalization, and doubts hovered in her conscience. Mimi had gotten along, but poorly at best. She was obviously neglected, if not only by herself, but by the forces that be. Any angle that she reasoned, it remained a constant that Mimi was a person who could use a lot of assistance, caring, and attention.

Now Mimi was entirely out of reach. There was no giving her a hand. There was no little favor that could soften Mimi's suffering. Mimi had vanished in a scorching burst of flame. To Zorra, it looked all too literally like a doorway to the mythical realms of Hell. Zorra could hear her father Frederico's voice booming, "Hell is no mythical place. It is as real as the nose on your face. It is more real than any pain or suffering you have ever known!" But Zorra did not perceive the legendary Heaven or Hell in a literal sense. Her father could pound tables until they collapsed into splinters, ferociously claiming that the existence of Hell was a known fact, but his passion had no impact on her mindset.

Both Heaven and Hell were to Zorra symbolic. *Symbolic,* to her, meant something left vague, a representation left unexplained, an implication not yet experienced, and therefore unknown. In the unreality of where Zorra now stood, she did not trust the reality of Mimi's disappearance. What Zorra did trust is that Mimi was suffering. She endeavored to hold onto hope, but found it hard to do so. Zorra's strongest hope was that Mimi had escaped.

Nobody dared to touch Mimi's old wheel chair. There were burn marks on the seat and the back, even along the arms of the chair. The singed shoes on the pale-lavender fur carpet became untouchable. The ghost of Mimi sat immortalized in the circle of black chairs like a shrine. Was it respect of the dead, or respect of the memory of Mimi that made us all unwilling to clean up the mess? I, for one, did not intend to step into the realm of spontaneous combustion. Who knows, maybe it's merely an unfortunate location in the room, like the Devil's Triangle, or the Bermuda Triangle. There were no volunteers among us to test my theory.

We gave Mimi three days to come back. Considering where we were, among the Doors to Other Worlds, we had no assurance that a missing-spontaneous-combustion-person might not just reappear in a burst of flame, dust a few ashes off, and carry on with her usual life. Not that Mimi had a usual life, but then, we were all living a bit beyond the usual, weren't we?

We decided to have a little ceremony for Mimi. A burial was not going to happen. That was lucky, because we hadn't run across any cemeteries behind the colored doors. Not yet, anyway. The ashes routine was a questionable consideration. Leave it to Eric to think up this one. He suggested scraping ashes off the chair and the shoes into one of the chalices from the banquet room. Zorra pointed out that ashes from a wooden chair and canvas shoes were not really the ashes of Mimi. Old Man Xavier added that none of us really wanted to touch the so called "scene of the crime," anyway.

We gathered on the fourth day after Mimi's spectacular disappearance in the room with the circle of black chairs. "Spectacular disappearance" had become the delicate terminology we had chosen so as to avoid words like death or incineration. Cynthia was there, along with Old Man Xavier, Eric, Zorra, and me. People we had seen at The Practitioner's waiting room showed up; the tired looking woman with her small girl, the stout man with the black beret, and the friendly old lady with the red dress, black shoes, pearls and white hair. The Practitioner himself

- 122 -

didn't make it, but his receptionist showed up wearing an aqua dress. This time her teased hair rolled like the letter S from her forehead and curled up in back. Her hair looked slightly less ridiculous now that she had removed her rectangular reading glasses.

Old Man Xavier had planned a little eulogy, not that he's a priest or anything, but he had his way with words. The two black chairs nearest The Shrine of Mimi were empty. Nobody wanted to sit in immediate proximity to the charred wheelchair and scorched shoes. Cynthia took the chair two seats to the right of the burn sight and Zorra took the chair two seats to the left. I noticed that the fish tank in the wall was covered with a miniature curtain.

Old Man Xavier cleared his throat, which served to quiet the chatter like a gavel in a courtroom. "We have gathered here in memory of..." I don't think he even reached mention of Mimi's name, when the miniature curtains opened with a zipping sound. We all turned to face the fish tank and in its place were puppets on strings lined up facing us. For me, this is now a memory that stands out, so let me take you back.

One of the puppets takes a step forward. He is dressed in orange with a yellow cape and a yellow cone shaped hat and a very long nose. "Ladies and gentlemen. Welcome! My name is Lord Devonshire, and I will be your host tonight. We have a delightful show for you tonight in honor of the Late Great Mimi."

From offstage right, a voice is calling, "Lord Devonshire, Lord Devonshire, stop the show. Hold everything!" Across the stage scurries a shaggy white dog-puppet. The shaggy dog approaches Lord Devonshire, "Please, Lord Devonshire, hold everything!"
The shaggy dog stops at Lord Devonshire's side, "Nonsense, Floppy, the show must go on."

"Arff, arff," yelps Floppy. "The Mademoiselle Mimi is putting on the last touches of her makeup."

"Well, yes, of course, Fluffy, or Floppy, whatever your name is," and Lord Devonshire turns this way and that before regaining composure. "No problem, really, the orchestra will be summoned to play a short overture."

Lord Devonshire and Floppy paddle off to the left while an old musician enters from the left. A backdrop lowers, concealing the repertoire of puppets. The backdrop is a pleasant city scene of several small-town buildings, a few rolling hills and street signs. The old musician wears an eyepiece in one eye, and a violin is tucked under his chin. He hobbles awkwardly onstage, his body bent forward from the waist. He scratches out an eerie tune that resembles the Funeral Procession a Marionette crossed with the Death March. His ominous sonata ends with the trailing of notes reminiscent of the Twilight Zone.

Someone in the audience applauds, but not enthusiastically, and Lord Devonshire reappears with a flourish of his yellow cape to introduce the main character, Miss Mimi Von Hertz. Mimi is a wiry little puppet in an olive green ankle-length dress, with her hair up in a bun and bright red lips. She wears a matching green jacket and totes a shiny black purse. As the story begins in the quaint little city, she is looking for work. She applies at *Freddy's Fast Cars,* a used car lot. Fast Freddy appears onstage with slicked back hair and a red and white striped short sleeve shirt. He's cool and casual. His business is booming. Little bright colored cars keep rolling by, each with an arm out the window and a fistful of money to hand over to Fast Freddy. Mimi is left waiting, application in hand, as Fast Freddy does a little song and dance about his Oh-So-Marvelous Cars and his Out-of-this-World Special Deals.

Finally, she is interviewed. "How fast can you type?" ….. "About fifty words per minute, Sir." ….."By the way, everybody just calls me Freddy. Can you count?"….. "Why of course, Sir, I mean Freddy." ….."Good. You look trustworthy. Start counting this cash," and Fast Freddy pushes a mountain of money in front of her.

Mimi lands the job as Fast Freddy's secretary. Not long after her hire day, a gentleman customer purchases a bright purple car and asks Mimi out on a date. The gentleman's name is Horace. Horace has on gray pants, an orange shirt, and a green tie. Horace takes Mimi out for a candlelight dinner with wine. He presents a ring to Mimi.

"Will you marry me, Mimi?" "Oh, my!" squeals Mimi. "Yes, I'll marry you."

Horace never touches another drop of wine, but he loves beer and he also loves whiskey, both in excess. Horace is no gentleman, as it turns out. He gets drunk and throws things at Mimi. A dish and a lamp and a chair fly across the stage. (You can see the puppet strings on the props, but the screaming and the crashing and banging are all well staged.)

Mimi shows up at work with a black eye and a bandaged arm. Fast Freddy's Cars are not selling so fast as the previous song-and-dance routine, so Fast Freddy gives Mimi a pink slip and lets her go. Mimi is distraught. If she tells Horace she has lost her job he will surely throw more furniture. She might end up in the hospital. She is nearly home when she discovers a big commotion. Her new house (where she lives with Horace) is on fire! A fireman informs her that her husband fell asleep smoking a cigarette, and he did not escape alive. As the fireman speaks, the roof caves in on the house. Now Mimi is not only jobless, she is homeless!

The old musician skittles across the stage, etching out another morose tune on his fiddle. Mimi reappears in rags pushing a shopping car. The yarn covered dog, Floppy, tags along behind her. (At least she has company.) Mimi sleeps on a park bench until a policeman wakes her and tells her to move along. She finds a hiding place behind a tree and sleeps there. When she wakes, rats are singing and dancing and hop-scotching all about her. Mimi screams. This part is the best acting in the whole puppet show, because this Mimi-character can sure let loose with a bone chilling scream.

The Rat Dance comes to its finale, and Mimi resumes pushing the shopping cart with Floppy tagging along behind her. Floppy has a cute little red, felt tongue hanging out and it's easy to imaging that he's panting. An energetic boy in baggy shorts and suspenders and a little baseball cap comes walking from the opposite direction and starts playing fetch-the-ball with Floppy. Mimi keeps pushing her shopping cart without noticing that Floppy is no longer tagging along.

A man in a black ski mask, pointing a hand gun, approaches Mimi. "Put your hands up, lady." Mimi does what she's told. "You may look poor, but I know you have a little money stashed somewhere in that shopping cart or in the pocket of your old sweater, don't you lady?" Mimi is terrified. She is shaking. "I don't have any money at all, Sir."

"I don't believe you," he retorts. "Give me all your money or I blow your brains out." The man points the gun at Mimi's face. Once again, she let's out that nerve rattling scream of hers. The man covers his ears and takes off running.

By now, Mimi sits on a bench and mumbles nonsense and jumbled thoughts to anyone who passes by. "I put the baby under the mattress. This cigarette is not a filter cigarette, do you hear me? Why would I bury all that money under my mother's garage? That's what he said, but that was a lie. It was a blue jay talking. He said the money is inside the baby. Your father is a baby. Your father is a big ol' baby. I don't have a filter cigarette. I told you, but you wouldn't listen."

The old musician shimmies onstage, playing a playful tune to accompany Mimi's nonsense. This is the best song he's played so far. A little bit of insanity adds a lot of zing to the music.

In the next scene, Mimi is propped up in a hospital bed. A nurse comes in to read stories to her. The nurse is smart. She has discovered that as long as she is reading aloud, Mimi gives up talking nonsense, and listens attentively. The nurse reads Jules Verne's *Journey to the Center of the Earth* and Fyodor Dostoyevsky's *Crime and Punishment*. (The nurse's reading selections may appear a little iffy for Mimi's condition, but obviously the patient is bedridden for a very long time. Fortunately, for the audience, this information is being narrated by Lord Devonshire.) The good news is that as long as the nurse reads there is no nonsense about mattresses and babies and filter cigarettes.

The nurse brings in another book called *The Unamusement Park*. The nurse's reading starts in with "You shouldn't have come here" and by the second or third page the nurse looks up. Mimi is not there in bed. The nurse sets down the book and throws up her arms, "It's a miracle. It's a miracle. Mimi has gone to the bathroom by herself!" But when the nurse goes to find Mimi, she is unable to find her anywhere. Little does she know that the place to find Mimi is described in the book she was reading, and Mimi is now walking down a hallway with a metal hoop full of old keys, past a red door, and now a blue door, and now a green door...

The old musician reappears onstage playing a dreadfully sinister tune, and the little curtain slowly pulls shut to mark the end of the puppet show.

THE CIRCULAR CLOSING

Old Man Xavier stands, applauding the puppet playhouse. He acknowledges that the funeral assembly must be tired and hungry, and therefore he condenses his eulogy. "What the marionettes demonstrated was a childlike version of Mimi Von Hertz' life. I met her years ago when she materialized in these hallways. I thank the nurse that read her the first few pages of *The Unamusement Park,* therefore sending Mimi into our lives. She was chosen as a guide for the transporter cells. Many of us have grown accustomed to calling these transporter cells by the more common name, glass marbles. Mimi had a variety of enchanting experiences here in our home of colored doors. She came out of hiding at numerous times during her stay here, leaving behind her mumble-jumble lingo, and in later years she would occasionally awake from her "deep sleep," capable of carrying on engaging conversations and, at rare moments, revealing the truly sensitive and loving creature that I know she is. Both worlds (the world outside, and the world in here) have a lot of sharp edges. We all have been damaged or injured along the way. Mimi passed through a series of tragic and brutal blows that bludgeoned her spirit and tore apart her nerves. She may have been grasping for rescue in the words that made so little sense to us. Eventually she abandoned her attempts at rescue and shut down completely, leaving us with a crumpled figure resigned to a wooden chair. I will not lead you to believe that Mimi has gone to a better place, or that she might be found in Heaven. I will not persuade you that Mimi found the way out of here, that she is the first to escape. I do not claim that Mimi is moving on to another life, her reincarnation. I choose to make no claims about the whereabouts of the Mimi I once knew.

I will tell you this. She touched my life as I know she touched many, and I will miss her as surely as all of you gathered here. Mimi, we keep you in our hearts and minds, in our dreams and hopes. We love you Mimi, and I hope that you hear our thoughts and prayers."

We all stood and gathered closer to form a circle by connecting hands. We stood a few moments, looking into each others eyes, with smiles and tears and the warmth of sharing this strange world together. The old woman with white hair and a red dress spoke these closing words, "Bless you, Mimi. Bless you."

BACK TO THE BOOB TUBE

Zorra is the most visibly affected by Mimi's absence. Eric tries to console her, catering to her as if she were a sick relative. Zorra grows irritable and even uninviting to Eric's attempts to soothe her pain. It takes several days for Eric to learn to steer clear of Zorra, allowing her to grieve and heal in solitude. As a result of their separation, I regain much of the companionship with Eric that had diminished after encountering Zorra. It is good for Eric, and good for me, that we can pal-around again. Nevertheless, after short lived adventures or a few philosophical rounds of the banquet table, Eric will become distracted, and needs to check on Zorra. After more episodes of feeling like a mouse battered by cat claws, Eric also falls into a slump. I can't tease him or cheer him up. He now longs for the old Zenith television, which is located in a section of the hall that is now locked off. We walk to the glass doorways and peer into the canvas covered hallway, but all of the old doors are unreachable. In fact, the cafeteria tables that we now frequent, are located in the contemporary, expansive section that we now have access to. The door to the new cafeteria room is paprika colored.

"Ask the glass marble to transport you to the apartment with the television," I suggest.

"Maybe you're not as dumb as you look," jests Eric, and I let him get away with it.

He pulls out his marble and holds it up to the light. After about ten seconds, I ask him, "Well, is it working?"

"Check it out, dude," he says with emphasis. I reach for his marble, but he reminds me to use my own. His memory is a little quicker, but we both recall that exchanging marbles resulted in exchanging identities.

I reminisce of the apartment we had camped out in, with its plastic covered recliner and its overdose of doilies scattered like snowfall. I am swiftly transported. Most of the room is still covered in sheets, as I had left it after my visionary dream. Eric is there on the white sheet covered couch and the Zenith set is already switched on with its drop-cloth pulled aside. I don't know where Eric found Tootsie Rolls, but that's what he's popping into his mouth, (the miniature, bite-size Tootsie Rolls that come in the economy bag). Already a litter-strewn mess of wrappers piles up on the coffee table. Eric seems to have the character of a chain smoker.

The news has gone from bad to worse. Two nuclear power plants malfunctioned within the same week. One was near New York City and the other was south of Los Angeles. There is no evidence, yet, of nuclear waste leaking, but then there was not yet evidence that there is not. An unidentified chemical is also detected in the large mass of water at Hoover Dam, and early tests by Biohazard Specialists are withheld by orders of the federal government as a precaution to avoid mass hysteria. The public has been informed that there is no immediate evacuation declared for any areas that gain access to water from the Colorado River. Public response, in various affected states, ranges from horrified to furious, from deeply concerned to those who see no need to over-react.

Since we last viewed the news there have been two more attacks on state capitols and another attempt on a military base. A crowd of people appear on the screen yelling, "The terrorists are here. The terrorists are among us."

There is a special report about a highly organized group of American teenagers, including some college students and even some high school students. These "kids" are thought to be linked by means of the World Wide Web, and have volunteered their services to a society that calls itself B.A.S.T.A.R.D.S. (Brothers and Sisters Turned to American Renegade Defense Strategy). These teenagers, the report claims, have become disillusioned with the insurmountable death, torture, disfigurement, and the disabling injuries of soldiers and civilians overseas. Adding to their disillusionment is the unending list of doomed or sacrificed hostages. As a result, the youngsters have turned against their own government, and they take action to defer recruitment and to disable the war effort. Patriots who support the troops call these youngsters traitors, but the teenagers claim that a traitor is a person who surrenders his life and the lives of others without questioning the orders of their elders.

According to a declaration made at the website, BASTARDS.com., war protests - as we have previously known, of a peaceful nature, have proven self-defeating and inefficient in turning the tides of heedless older generations, who keep sending their own children and grandchildren to war. These teenagers believe that the current military effort abroad has succeeded to antagonize and encourage the mushrooming growth of terrorism, and at the same time has succeeded to decay our own national security as well as international security. BASTARDS.com is a "collective call to action for young people who intend to disarm the war effort, the youth slaughter, and the humiliating display of our own country's terrorism in other countries."

"I remember during the Vietnam War, when disapproval of the war was expressed by draft dodgers who crossed the border into Canada," I interject.

"It really didn't stop the war, did it? It was only a way for someone to save his own neck," responds Eric.

"This group called BASTARDS.com has chosen to harm our own people. I think they are over-reacting," I claim.

"Over-reacting? A bunch of old geezers in the congress and the white house decide to sacrifice my neck overseas. They offer me a job to go murder people. They coerce my friends to go mess up the rest of their lives. Have you ever looked at all the Vietnam War veterans out on the street begging for spare change? Do the congressmen and the white house geezers give them the time-of-day now? I say leave me and my buddies out of it. Go fight your own battles. But this organization, BASTARDS.com, goes one step beyond that. Instead of saying, *go fight your own battles*, they are saying stop fighting the battles. Why do you think terrorist attack us? It's not because we were so good and stayed home and minded our own business. Do you see terrorist attacks in Switzerland, a country that remains neutral?"

"You've got a point there. In fact, Eric, you've got a pretty good head on your shoulders." I say this with sincerity, but I also feel that a little flattery might calm him down. He's getting really worked up about it, but then, I have to say, I don't blame him.

The news starts to repeat itself. The latest disasters are described again. Contrasting claims are made by politicians about the initiators of the attacks. More footage of the war abroad fills up the screen. I get up and click off the television. "Let's go get some food, or go for a walk," I suggest. "You wanted to watch the boob tube to cheer up, but the world-out-there is getting you more upset. You'd be better off watching MTV."

"Hey, I was trying to forget about Zorra, and it worked, O.K.?"

I nod. We get up, ready to exit the room. Eric reaches into his pocket for his glass marble, and I recall that we are only in this apartment as a result of the transporter cells. In this apartment, we are now like characters in a book – a book that we have decided to close and put aside. Actually, we are both standing at the glass doors that separate us from the old canvas-covered hallway. We put the transporter cells back into our pockets, turn around and head down the expansive new hallway toward the paprika colored door for a bite to eat. What's going through my mind is an odd thought that I decide not to tell Eric. Instead of saying that the real world is a mess, and he'd be better off watching MTV, I am thinking that maybe he is better off in this weird hallway full of colored doors and bazaar experiences. To me, reality doesn't look inviting enough to merit escape from here.

THE TAN DOOR

The color of the new door that we enter requires this brief explanation. In a mindset of tanning booths or summers-on-the-beach, the word *tan* might mean a copper-brown or deeper shade of flesh. The words *flesh tone* might bring to mind a creamy-white, tinged with pink. But *flesh tone,* in respect to the epidermis of Homo sapiens, covers a wide spectrum of colors. The tan door that Eric and I now enter is a creamy white shade of beige.

Our first few steps are apprehensive, as we find ourselves in a narrow corridor lined with wooden plank shelves. On both sides are three shelves of bare heads, each with a neck, and all lined up in rows, each with one ear facing us. One shelf is level with my shoulder, the middle shelf is level with my hip, and the lower shelf is at my ankle. We feel a slight sense of alarm, naturally, but we both have gone shopping for Halloween costumes frequently enough to have seen a similar sight. We are, therefore, willing or hopeful to discover that the heads are made of rubber, a mere simulation of a horrible practice. (Apparently, somebody is collecting and cataloging human heads, or somebody wants us to believe this). I don't quite muster the nerve to touch any one of the heads, which would serve as a reliable test. Human skin does feel completely unlike rubber.

I say *collecting and cataloging* because each head has a metal tag (piercing the earlobe and angled awkwardly – not dangling like an earring). On the tag is a series of digits and dashes and letters. One tag reads WS-279-351. Every head is clean shaven, hairless, and with closed eyelids. These heads are Anglo-Saxon heads, and the flesh tones range only slightly from the color of the tan door. There were a few moles, scars, and no shortage of freckles and wrinkles, although most have smooth unblemished skin.

The corridor is only about twenty feet long, and ahead of us, through an open doorway, is a larger room, emitting incandescent blurs of yellow, red, blue, green, and violet that move within a pitch black space. These lights appear inviting, but in consideration of the disturbing display of severed heads, we stop dead in out tracks and consider turning back. Who in their right mind would walk like a lamb to their slaughter, given a fair enough premonition that decapitation awaits them?

"I'm not getting a good feeling about this place, Eric," I comment.

"Yeah, it's kind of creepy. You know what I'm thinking, though? No matter how creepy or horrifying this might be, it's not real. Like, when the Lady Insect Goddess ripped off my family jewels, I was horrified, but later on I realized that it didn't really happen. Believe me, everything is still intact down there. All this stuff in here is really just messin' with our minds. When the ride's over, everything is A – OK, like a visit to the haunted house."

I take a deep breath. Obviously, Eric wants to experience this room ahead of us.

We advance gingerly into the dark room with its motion of colored lights. Rock stars must feel like this, up on a dark stage, blinded by stage lights covered with color-gels. As my eyes adjust, I see that the lights are not in beams, like a flashlight. The glowing colors seem more like floating fists or tennis balls. Maybe they are large fireflies of various hues. Another doorway stands ahead of us, with angled amber light spilling toward us. The roomful of colored fireflies is not alarming, it is pleasant, but it is also dark and we are unsure of where we step.

Through the doorway full of beaming light we pass into what appears to be a theater lobby. There are marble benches with engraved embellishments, and red velvet drapery, pulled into large swooping curves. Eric starts chuckling behind me and I turn to see him clowning around like an orangutan. He spreads his arms slightly and they appeared elongated, as if they nearly reach his feet without bending. He walks with a rocking, Frankenstein motion, stiff-legged, tilting left and then right. He is really enjoying himself. His face takes on a goofy smile and I am certain that his head has become pie shaped. His features flattened into a round disc. He tilts his body to the left, and tips his head to the left. His whole face rolls like a large coin down his shoulder and long arm, turning upside down and then sideways until he catches it with his hand. Upon his hand, his head is angled upside down, while his eyes look this way and that. He then shift his weight from left to right, and his head rolls back up the arm, across the shoulder, and down the other arm to be caught by the right hand, where it lands sideways. As his pie face is rolling, he makes a ridiculous "whoa-ooo" sound that accentuates the loops that are drawn with his mouth. The poor guy has no neck, but after rolling his head back and forth two times he rolls it back up to his shoulders. He steps toward me and he has now returned to his usual proportions, shorter arms and an oval face resting on a neck.

I feel a little hoodwinked, as if I've befriended a boy who seems to be some manufactured contortionist. Eric looks like his usual self again. He speaks with an old English accent, "You must get ahead in life." He grabs hold of his ears, pops off his head, and bumps his head into mine. My head is knocked off my shoulders, landing with a thud on the red carpet. Eric places his head, facing backwards, on my shoulders, so I flip it forward with my hands. Filled with hysteria, I look for my own head, which I find on the floor behind me - yelling, unhappy, and making a fuss. Headless Eric picks up my head and tries it on for size. We look at each other and have a good laugh. We laugh until tears come to our eyes. I'm not sure which one of us is Eric and which one is me, but the Eric-body-with the-Jacob-head points to a corner of the lobby near one of the marble benches. My body (with Eric's head) looks over my shoulder. There stands a tall fish tank of colorful creatures, all restless and shifting positions. This Unamusement Park sure does seem to specialize in underwater displays.

We cross the lobby for a better inspection, and the fish tank is truly a strange one. There are miniature animals with human heads swimming and playing in the bubbling water. A tiny snow owl sports the head of The Practitioner. A little white cat has a miniature Zorra face with flowing black hair. A dragonfly, about a foot long, has the tiny face of Old Man Xavier with his long gray beard. A swallow swoops gracefully through the water with a miniature Eric face wearing a backwards ball cap, and a small brown rabbit doing the frog swim with my own tiny head and face. One of the creatures moves like an eel, its body maneuvering switchback curves with the tiny face of Mimi, her eyes tightly shut, as usual. Drifting calmly in the water is an elegant jellyfish. With a pulsing movement it opens like a parachute to reveal the face of Cynthia. On the candy colored pebbles at the bottom there is a ruby-red hermit crab, whose legs peek out from its shell followed by the petite face of the receptionist, with her little black rimmed glasses and her teased hair in a tightly plastered swirl.

Head swapping is not something I would have dreamed up. Who is making this happen? As Eric would say, who is messin' with our heads here? And if this is the action in the theater lobby, I don't believe I want to know what's going on in the theater!

THE TRAILER PARK

I manage to convince Eric to postpone the theater show, (or is it Eric's head convincing mine that we should leave?) At any rate, we retreat through the radiant firefly room and exit through the corridor of catalogued heads. We are a sight to behold, a man and a teenager with swapped heads. I have no idea what to expect, or how we are planning to switch heads back. The House of Mind Games is obviously a maze of unexpected experiences, and I am growing more capable of leaving logic behind. I become less inclined to seek interpretations of these experiences. When we step back outside the tan door, I see Eric's head on Eric's body, and I know that I am back to "normal." (How might I avoid using such an overly vague term - *normal*?)

Eric and I may be back to "normal," but the hallway is playing tricks on us. We stand on a small blue carpeted platform with several stairs that descend to an asphalt street. We stand outside on the porch in front of a mobile home with a tan door. Across the street is another mobile home, its door is charcoal gray. There are mobile homes in consecutive rows, each arranged evenly with equal sized lots. The lots are barely large enough for displaying a small row of potted plants. The doors vary in color. In fact, the mobile homes vary in color and décor. Some have striped awnings above their side windows, and others have window boxes of flowers or cactuses. The mobile home park would not impress me as anything abnormal, or exceptional, had I stepped out of this door three years ago.

Today, though, considering the sequence of extraordinary events since being handed my ring full of keys, I perceive the mundane geometry of the park layout with a heightened sense of intrigue. I think that I would feel the same about a mobile home park, even if I were back outside of the House of Mind Games. There is, beyond a shadow of a doubt, and incited by a new awareness, something unique behind every door. Each mobile home is a shell that holds separate families, separate cultures, separate realities, and separate perceptions of the world and its people.

I have my usual panicky feeling that I'm being hoodwinked again, but I know better than to anticipate the nature of my new discoveries. This is a wonderful feeling, and I want to staple it onto the bulletin board of my consciousness. I hope that for the remainder of my life, I will be able to draw upon such openness. It is invigorating to perceive that anything is possible, that a new experience is not necessarily a disaster, threatening to rob me of my "safety zone" of reliable repetition.

Maybe I will meet a Hindu family from India, or an old couple from Missouri. Perhaps I will meet a mixed couple, one African and the other Arabian, or perhaps I will meet a hip-hop teenager. Maybe I will encounter someone gay, or handicapped, or psychic, or introverted. Why on earth would I consider myself so "special" that I feel a need to protect myself from such glorious diversity? I have a new sense of adventure about the human race. I am convinced that my elementary school teachers have instilled in me a sense of wonder about the variety of cultures and individuals of the planet. A dialogue of idealism still exists in my awareness, but the feeling of enthusiasm and awe had been whittled down over the years. The reality of seeing cultures clash, of witnessing how bigotry causes suffering and mistrust, of living with the harshness we see between the *haves* and the *have-nots* – so many difficulties have beaten upon my sense of wonder. A protective force field of my own creating has grown out of adulthood, and I have allowed the force field to dim my outlook, to fog over the glasses that I look through, observing the people around me. It is not stupidity that leads me to avoid the alley of loud drunks, to cross the street to the other side, away from confrontational-tough-guys who look like reckless drug hustlers and ex-cons. Intuition has served me for my own protection and survival. Somehow along the way, and this is the unfortunate part, I have allowed my instinct for protection and survival to outweigh the possibilities of opportunities. I have learned to avoid almost everyone. Everyone has become too risky for me, too unpredictable, too dangerous. They are all too human. I have allowed myself to close up like an oyster. I seem to be living by a strict code of non-commitment. And here are the rules: 1. Don't get too involved. 2. Don't get sidetracked. 3. Don't be persuaded. 4. Don't put my emotions on the line. Somehow I have become my own radio frequency, and I have tuned everybody else out. I'm exaggerating, of course, but not much.

But at this moment, with a surprise view of a common trailer park, something in my psyche (or my heart, or my spirit, I'm not sure which) has shifted. I feel lighthearted and optimistic. I feel an eagerness to explore this mobile home park. Believe me, this is a radical shift, a profound change of heart. Isn't a mobile home resident commonly synonymous with "lowlife?" (Oh, I know…mobile home parks are full of kindly old folks who, having spent decades serving society, are now retired to a simpler life.) But trailer parks are no symbol of great achievement or of monetary success. Here I stand on a wobbly little porch, anxious to explore the possibilities.

To my surprise, Eric is not interested. He takes one look at the trailer park and feels disheartened, convinced that he might never see Zorra again. "How will we ever find her if the hallway has disappeared?" he complains.

I look at him in amazement. "On the other side of the door you were happy to juggle your head like a basketball, and swapping heads was all fun and games, but now the sight of a trailer park depresses you. And just when I get all enthusiastic!" I point out.

"It's not the trailer park that's depressing me. It's the thought of never seeing Zorra again," he clarifies.

"OK, I've got an idea. Pull out your glass marble, transporter cell, and think of the whereabouts of Zorra right now," I suggest.

"Duh!! Why didn't I think of that?" he smiles vaguely as he reaches into his pants pocket. He holds the marble up to the light of the blue sky, and after a few moments his smile fades and he sits down on the porch step.

"Couldn't you locate her?" I asked him.

"She's asleep on a couch in a room full of couches, but I never saw that room before."

"Can you see the color of the door?"

"Not really. I see Zorra and a few couches, but that's all I see."

"Tell you what. Spend a few minutes with me, checking out this mobile home park, and maybe after a half an hour she will be awake and you'll be able to locate her."

"I was thinking I'll just sit here and watch her, but maybe you're right. I can always check on her in twenty minutes or so."

He stands up, pockets the marble, and we bounce down the steps to the road, looking to decide which trailer to start with.

As it turns out, we don't have to select a door. A door seems to select us. A spicy mustard colored door opens and an industrious looking woman in a soft floral print dress steps out on her porch to shake out a throw rug. The woman's skin was pitch-black and she is very slender, with bright eyes and coral lipstick. Her hair is twirled into a coil on the top of her head. The throw rug is shag blue, and she smiles at us as she drapes the rug over the porch rail. "Hello boys, are you hungry? I just baked some cherry pie and I have some vanilla bean ice cream, just waiting to be scooped up and slapped on the tops of three slices."

"Sounds cool to me," blurts out Eric.

I am perfectly happy to not have to persuade Eric, especially now that calorie counting is left behind - far, far away in a strange place called reality.

The friendly woman signals to us to come on over, disappearing into the trailer and leaving her spicy mustard colored door wide open. We clamored up the pale green steps. Her voice calls out to us, "Come on in, boys." Her doorway is draped with long strings of beads of yellow, gold, white, black, and ochre. Small bells at the ends of the strings tinkle and chime as we step into her colorful abode. On the floor rests a cross-section of a large tree stump, with stubby legs. It makes a low table for sitting on the floor. Dried grass mats are arranged around the table for seating on the deep blue shag rug. The walls are a dark rust or red clay color. Displayed on the walls are fiberglass cases with a variety of elaborate hats - hats from the nineteen twenties, and hats from the seventeen hundreds.

The cheery woman appears from her kitchen carrying a silver tray with a cherry pie, a tub of ice cream, wooden spoons and dark brown clay baked plates. She catches us gaping at her hat collection. "They call me the Hat Lady. It's very rare for newcomers to meet me bareheaded. I'm always seen out and about with a large hat on," she smiles with a true radiance, kneels down to place the tray on the round table, and excuses herself to return to the kitchen for a pie cutter and some fresh tea. She returns with a wooden tray, carrying a spherical pitcher of tea with flower petals floating in it. The tea mugs are blue frosted glass with dolphin handles, and the silver pie cutter has a cockatiel engraved in the handle.

"My name is Hatshepsut, after the Queen of Egypt, but my friends all call me Hatty."

"My name is Jacob, and this is my buddy Eric," I turn to the wiz kid, busy stuffing his face with cherry pie. Eric smiles a comical smile, his cheeks puffed up like a chipmunk.

"Pleased to meet you, Jacob and Eric."

Eric just nods, so I respond, "The pleasure is ours. You are very hospitable."

Hatty smiles gracefully, spooning up a dab of vanilla bean ice cream with one warm cherry for herself.

An older woman's voice calls from outside the mobile home, "Hatty, oh, Hatty, are you home, dear?"

"Pardon me, gentlemen," Hatty places her clay plate gently and silently on the table. Without the support of her arms she rises up from her cross-legged position as gracefully as a ballerina.

I notice in the floral pattern of her loose dress, a few sprigs of ripe cherries. I can imagine her feet in red heels and a large-brimmed red hat, swooping over one eye. I can see in her the elegance of a fashion model.

She hurries to the doorway, and with one hand on the doorframe, she leans outside, "Amelia, is that you, sweetie? I've just baked a fresh pie and you must taste it. Come on up, I have a surprise for you."

"Oh, Hattie, you're always baking, and yet you stay as thin as a rail," Hatty steps backward, and a stately matriarch steps into the modest room, parting the hanging beads with white gloved fingers spread wide. I have no formal background or experience with the intricate etiquette of the well-to-do or aristocratic society, but I find myself rising to me feet, preparing to bow. Even more amazing, I see that Eric has followed my example.

"Amelia, may I present my new acquaintances, Jacob and his young companion, Eric."

"How do you do?" greets Amelia, extending her hand, palm down, as if preparing for a kiss on the hand. Amelia stands in the doorway with her outstretched hand, and I decipher that I am required to cross the room to take her hand.

"How do I do what?" inquires Eric.

I pass behind Eric as he says this, jabbing him with my elbow. "It's a pleasure to meet you," I say crossing the room to take her hand.

Up close, Amelia is quite a shock to look at. I feel as though *Ambush Makeover* has gotten hold of the *Wicked Witch of the West*. Amelia's eyes are piercing and demanding, in boldly drawn mascara, and made all the more severe by two thin eyebrows etched high on her bulging forehead. Her dark curls, piled high and laced with golden ribbons and green berries, might have looked more delicate on a young maiden.

"Likewise, I'm sure," she chirps, dismissing me like a trite commoner.

Eric approaches her next, taking her hand, "My name is Eric."

"What a strong name for a messy little boy," she responds, pulling her hand away.

"Amelia, the pie is delicious. Have a piece, sweetie," Hattie jumps in to smooth things over. "I'll fetch you a chair."

"Just a sliver, Hattie."

Amelia directs her attention to the hat display as Hattie goes to the kitchen. I make note of the outfit that Amelia is wearing. The shoulders are padded, almost pointed, and she's wearing metallic green stretch pants that disappear into her low black heels.

Hattie reappears with a wooden chair. Amelia seats herself delicately, with both legs off to one side, as if riding sidesaddle.

"Look, it's snowing outside!" declares Eric, pointing to the small window, with chartreuse curtains drawn wide.

"It never snows here," responds Hattie, and we all move toward the bright window, all except Amelia, who remains posed in her chair.

"The snowflakes look like torn up paper," I comment, heading for the front door, tilting my head back for an eyeful of sky.

"Oh my lord," cries Hattie. "Ashes are falling from the sky!"

Sure enough, the bushes, mailboxes, flower boxes are strewn with a powdery layer of dust mixed with flakes of white and charcoaled ash. A dark hood of midday gloom mysteriously sheds free floating confetti, reminding me of shreds of calendar pages tossed twirling and glittering from the office windows of skyscrapers on New Years Day. The sun, like a cutout hole in the clouds, is a radiation shade of pink. Every visible window glows metallic green, reflecting the strange powdery landscape in silvery mirrors.

"Is there a volcano nearby?" Eric inquires.

"Not to my knowledge," responds Hattie, crossing the room. She extends the antenna on a portable radio on the bookshelf, and clicks on the volume knob. We all wince at the eardrum-piercing roar of static. She lowers the volume and spins the frequency knob until a woman's voice comes over the airwaves, "A cluster of brushfires is spreading quickly through Eden Ranch, Arroyo Seco, and the foothills of Mustang Park. Northwesterly gusts of wind are fueling these fires and causing the flames to travel swiftly and dangerously from these remotely populated areas into the densely populated suburbs of Alta Vista, Briar Creek Canyon, and Granite Heights. We will have a report, momentarily, from Fire Chief Anderson concerning evacuations and rescue efforts. These brushfires are, as I now speak, not yet contained, and we are receiving numerous calls from residents experiencing the fallout of thick ash, from as far west as Lake Sutro, and as far north as Remington. We are being advised that if you live in an area that is not within immediate danger, or an area that is not being evacuated, to please remain inside. The air quality is extremely poor. If you absolutely must go outside, or if you are driving, it is recommended that you cover your nose and mouth with a cloth or painter's mask. Do not turn on your air conditioner. I repeat, do not use your air conditioner. The soot in the air is thick and may be harmful to your lungs and your eyes."

"How dreadful," moans Amelia, still side-saddling the wooden chair, and rolling a cherry around her plate with a fork.

Eric forms an image in his mind of Amelia, tied to a chair with her fork and plate, and locked into a closet. He can picture us leaving her behind to burn up in the fire. His eyes sparkle and a sly grin crosses his face, and I can guess that he's enjoying her discomfort.

"We mustn't lose our heads," says Hattie calmly.

"Speaking of lost heads, I have an idea," blurts out Eric. "Maybe if we go back to the trailer with the tan door, and return back to the collection of earmarked heads, we'll be back in the Hallway of Mind Games, and we'll be safer there."

"You might be right Eric," I respond. "Swapping heads or even juggling heads might be preferable to going up in flames." We have presupposed, here, that exchanging one illusion for another will protect us from the danger of the first.

Hattie curls one side of her lower lip and raises her eyebrows with a look of questionable disbelief. Amelia stands, placing her plate and fork on the seat of the wooden chair. From the looks of things, we are all preparing for an exodus to the strange head swapping lounge behind the tan door.

"Wait!" demands Hattie. "I cannot bear to abandon my hat collection." She pulls a small key from her dress pocket. The key opens the side panels of fiberglass that encase her precious hats on the wall. "If we each wear one hat, and carry two, we should be able to save them all."

The Kodak moment that follows is both comical and dramatic. The four of us cross the street like drag queens returning from a shopping spree. High fashion hats, a circus carnival of colored felt, feathers, satins, brocaded ribbons, jewels, furry tails, tatted webs, and diaphanous veils, caravan beneath a dark horror-story sky of descending snowflake-ashes that collect on our shoes, shoulders and hat brims. On the backside of the photo will be this slogan in cursive, *Shop 'til You Drop*.

We climb the tiny stairway-porch to the tan door, and pass like disrespectful clowns between rows of bare heads. Stepping single file into the firefly room, Eric makes a miraculous observation. In the dark room of bustling colored light, one red lightning bug turns into a doorway that we hadn't noticed earlier.

"Hey, look at this!" Eric calls us over to a doorway near the one we just passed through. We follow him into another tight corridor, with shelves on both sides stocked with more of the same, catalogued heads. We would not have guessed that this was a different corridor, had we not just made a U turn. Eric leads the way past the heads to another tan door, and turns to us with crossed fingers, before turning his back and reaching for the knob. I'm excited, realizing that he will be reunited with Zorra, and we all can see Cynthia and Old Man Xavier again.

When Eric pulls the door open, we all said "Oooh," and "Ahhh," and "Wow," simultaneously. Behind this tan door is a Magritte sky full of cloud puffs on robin-egg blue. Dispersed among the clouds in an arrangement like fruit on an invisible tree, there floats a spectrum of colored doors. Not one of us considers stepping into such a surreal scene. How does one walk on sky? Why bother to open a door, if you can already see the sky behind it? Most likely, we have allowed our engrained logic, or sense of reason, to deter us from a magical experience. In addition to our reticence, Eric is (as you might say) a man on a mission. These doors in the clouds do not appear to lead back to Zorra.

Eric closes the tan door, and we back out of the corridor of shelved heads. In the dark room full of flying lights, Eric catches sight of yet another open doorway, very near the last one. Once again we enter a new corridor, single-file, and once again are were shelves full of documented, clean shaven heads. With all of our wild hats, it occurs to me that head swapping might become quite comical. I mention this to Hattie.

"I wouldn't object to a little bit of disciplined head swapping, but if we start rolling heads around like bowling balls, I would demand that all hats be removed," she responds.

Eric and I burst out laughing, but I don't think Amelia is amused. At the end of this storeroom of heads is a third tan door. There are so many storage rooms full of skinheads that I feel as if we were touring the catacombs of a graveyard. This time, before turning the doorknob, Eric turns toward us with two sets of crossed fingers. I have to admit that I too have my fingers crossed. The tan door swings open, and low and behold, there is the contemporary hallway Eric and I know so well.

"So this is the famous Hallway of Mind Games you two have been talking about," Hattie states quizzically.

"Not only that," I inform her, under my breath, "This is where Eric left his sweetheart."

Eric looks back at us with a look of resolve in his eyes, but the twenties flapper hat pulled over his ball cap detracts from any real seriousness to his determination.

With the help of my transporter cell, I locate Cynthia. She has developed a highly sophisticated doll house, a miniature castle with royalty, lords and ladies, and of course a prince and princess. The castle has servants and guards, with a fanfare of trumpeters in puffy red pants, white stockings, and red pin-cushion hats. A drawbridge allows passage over the moat. A knight in shining armor can be found riding a white stallion on a path through the surrounding forest.

Old Man Xavier is located in a sensory deprivation tank, floating like a sleeping crocodile in murky green water. No doubt, his meditations and hallucinations are evolving far beyond our rookie experiences.

Eric manages to visit Zorra and returns looking like he had just seen a ghost. (Compared to any experience here at the House of Mind Games, a ghost might not seem very frightening.) Eric face, however, is pale and his eyes appear to be dilated. He holds in his hand Zorra's ivory necklace of bear claws and hawk talons.

"Is Zorra alright?" I ask, fearing the worst.

"She must be sick or depressed or malnourished or something," Eric responds with concern. "She sleeps most of the day. At night, apparently, she doesn't sleep well. I found her little hideaway in a roomful of couches. I sat with her for a while, her head in my lap, stroking her hair. I tried to encourage her with the usual words – everything's going to be OK, you'll get better, you'll see. I even promised to get her out of here one day."

"She fell asleep and I noticed her ivory necklace peeking out from under the couch. I picked it up, thinking of it as some sort of Native American talisman or good luck charm. I even said a prayer for Zorra, holding the necklace like a rosary. When I opened my eyes, a very grotesque idea came to my mind as I looked at the necklace."

Eric holds the necklace up close to me, "Does this look to you like what I think it is?"

I take the necklace in my hand, surprised at the weight of it. All of the carved ivory looks like bones, and there is a depiction of a bird's claw, along with the paw of wolf or bear, but I now see what Eric is referring to. Placed evenly between claws and talons, there are the bones of fingers.

"It looks like human fingers," I respond. "But Eric, ivory tusks could be filed into the shape of fingers. I don't think they're real," I say, downplaying it. The truth is that I am lying in an attempt to calm Eric down.

"Touch them, Jacob," he almost whispers. "Touch them."

I feel the knuckle joints and run my own fingertip along the length of one bone. It is dry and brittle like real bone, and I can't deny that. "Maybe you're right, Eric. But surely, a dead person has no concern for his lost bones."

"What if the person is not dead?" Eric holds my gaze with a solemn urgency.

I remember then, the story Eric had told me about his abusive father, and of his brother who had known hostages whose fingers were severed, one day at a time. No wonder Eric is spooked. The necklace looks like evidence of one of the worst horror stories Eric has ever heard, and the story was told by his older brother, a returned soldier.

"For all we know, Zorra may have purchased this necklace at a jewelry store," I point out.

"For all we know, Zorra is from a tribe of savages known for torturing people and keeping the amputated bones as souvenirs," Eric responds.

"Did you ask her?" I ask.

"She was asleep on my lap. Besides, if she is one of the savages, she will surely lie to cover her tracks." Eric postulates.

"I'll talk to her about it, OK? If you look a person directly in the eye, you have good chance of detecting a lie in the making. To tell the truth, though, Zorra does seem like a person who wouldn't hurt a fly."

"That's exactly the way I perceive Zorra, but the necklace still gives me the heebie-jeebies," said Eric wincing.

SQUIRREL CAGE

Hattie and Amelia are newcomers to our Unamusement Park. I promote myself to the position of tour guide. Many of my experiences and much of my knowledge of the Hallway of Colored Doors belonged to the older hallway, still under renovation. I would have loved to show them the aquarium in the floor, and find out what fanciful creatures emerged from their metamorphosis in the swimming pool. Paradise is, of course, a place worth showing every tourist. And to tell the truth, I missed the old medieval banquet table. We now have a large cafeteria, its walls lined with vending machine. Actually, the term "vending" is entirely a misnomer. True, these machines are push-button, with packaged foods displayed behind a thick glass. There is, however, no bill or coin-insertion mechanism. The food and drinks are absolutely complimentary. So far, I have yet to pass behind a single doorway in this House of Mind Games that requires a ticket, a payment, or any sort of currency, credit card, IOU, or personal check. One advantage, to be sure, of leaving reality behind, is the complete absence of waiting in line for a stranger to write out a personal check (not to mention the elaborate delay of check approval). And you know you've either died or gone to La-La Land if you never have to pay a red cent. Living without money feels somewhat like life without the devil. But as you know, we cannot discern if we are lost in somebody's imagination, trapped in our own unending dream, or held captive in some kid's video game. This uncertainty prompts an uneasiness that all but blots out the advantage of a free ride.

I take Hattie and Amelia to the room with circle of black chairs. Immediately, Hattie is curious about the blackened wheelchair and charred shoes. When Amelia turns from the fish tank to look at the shrine of Mimi, she screams in a whimpering voice, and faints, landing with a dull thud on the thick blue shag rug. Hattie darts across the room to her friend, sliding into a kneeling position as if she were stealing base. She frantically fans the poor passed-out woman with her wide brimmed hat, while I run to fetch a cup of water. Amelia is moaning by the time I return from the hallway, and Hattie dips her fingers in the plastic cup I hold, sprinkling cool water on Amelia's forehead.

Amelia stirs slightly, and Hattie pats her cheeks. When Amelia opens her eyes, she says, "Take me from this dreadful place. Please take me away from here." Hattie and I help her up and support her as we exited the high curtained room.

"I'm sorry, I guess I was hoping there would be a puppet show, but it's only the fish tank now," I try smoothing things over, lest they think I'm a poor tour guide.

"No, dear, the fish aquarium was lovely, but that burned up chair gave me a dreadful fright," replies Amelia, still leaning heavily on our arms.

I notice that Amelia has a habit of using the word dreadful. Maybe this choice of word was revealing some quality of her nature or outlook. At any rate, I discreetly omit any explanation about our incinerated friend Mimi. The shrine left to a visible case of spontaneous combustion rates very high on the itinerary of my tour, but apparently Amelia has a weak stomach, a weak heart, or a weak constitution.

Seeing that Amelia is feeling light-headed, I pull out my transporter cell to locate Zorra or Eric, because I remember Eric speaking about a roomful of couches. I locate Zorra asleep on a couch, but the sight of her in my crystal ball is of no help. I need to know the color of the door to the couch room. I then locate Eric in the cafeteria with a bowl of melted cheddar cheese and jalapenos. He dips Fritos into the bright yellow guck, a teenager's simulation of Nachos. I take the ladies to the cafeteria. Fortunately, the couch room is very near, behind a satiny white door. Hattie, Amelia, and I sit across from Eric, who offers to share his bag of Fritos. "That looks disgusting. I have no appetite at all," responds Amelia. Hattie selects a green apple from one of the wall machines. Eric informs me that the couch room has a brass colored door. We decide that the roomful of couches is a good enough destination for all of us, and head out for the brass door.

Zorra is still there. We try to enter quietly so as no to awake her. Despite our efforts, she sits up, looking a little disoriented, disheveled, and embarrassed. "Pardon us, Zorra, for intruding on you, but our friend Amelia fainted earlier. We thought she might recuperate here on a sofa."

"Hi, Jacob. Hi, Eric. Hello, everyone," Zorra pulls her long hair back away from her face.

"My name is Hattie," and I witness Hattie introducing herself with her hat on, as she had mentioned in her trailer.

"Hello, my name is Zorra," and the two shake hands while I prop up a cushion from another sofa to form a pillow for Amelia, who stretched out like a hospital patient. Eric sits in the vicinity of Zorra, but not the same couch. Hattie selects a couch of her own. She busies herself by chewing on her green apple. I, too, decide to stretch out on a couch and relax. I close my eyes and the room is silent.

....

I am a passenger on a bus. The bus seems to be a school bus, but the passengers are adults. We pass through a few tree-lined residential streets. The bus stops at a hillside park. We disembark, and scatter randomly up the hill. This park is very dry, a desert slope. I'm more than halfway up the hill, feeling somewhat separated from the other adults who have joined me on this outing. The terrain alters dramatically. There are lush green reeds up to my shoulders, and sparkling blue water spilling over boulders and my feet and lower legs are under water. The tall reeds are so dense that only occasional spills of water are visible, and I panic with confusion, wondering where I can step safely without being swept away by the rushing water. The entire hill is a river flooding the overgrown grass.

Fortunately, I locate an octagon shaped building, its windows forming a circle, and its roof a flat disc. I enter a hallway. The walls are brick and the metal doors are painted mud beige. Inside the first door to the left is bald man across the room. The bald man seems dangerous. He is yelling at somebody around a corner. I cannot see who he is yelling at, but the bald man behaves like a psycho. He is demonic and treacherous. I exit the room, apparently unseen. I feel like a coward because there is somebody around the corner who needs to be rescued from the psychotic bald man. I leave them both behind.

In the hallway are two spiders the size of Dungeness crabs, one red and one black. The spider legs look armored, like crab legs, and the crablike walking gives me the chills. One of these spiders could wrap its legs entirely around my head – a very unpleasant thought. The spiders are headed to the left, so I walk briskly to the right.

I wake up in the dark. The cushion beneath my head is soaked with sweat. My hair, too, is wet. I realize, in the darkness, that I am with a roomful of odd companions. These companions are the phantoms or holograms of an unreal, imaginary, lost world. Why do I feel so safe with these new found friends? I've just woken from a disturbing nightmare, and I feel an assurance that these people sleeping on couches are all real. We have been thrown together so randomly. The truth is, though, that I could say that for the so-called *real world* outside these strange walls. In my "real life", we are also thrown together so randomly.

If this House of Mind Games is all a dream, I just had a nightmare within a dream. It's like a reflection inside a reflection inside a reflection, ad infinitum. Speaking of reflections, what about that first door to the old hallway, with its mirror that I chose not to step through?

Along with the absence of money, this place has a deliberate absence of time clocks. Even the old lady's Felix-the-Cat clock is utterly unreliable. But clock or no clock, I remember the bygone nights, waking up at three in the morning, my mind spinning like a squirrel cage. That's exactly the way I feel at this moment, like its three a.m., and my thoughts are racing out of control.

Old Man Xavier pays us a visit in the room full of couches early that morning. He's dressed himself up in a magician's tuxedo, with a top hat and tails, and even a black wand with a white tip. "Is it Halloween?" wonders Eric.

"All Hallows Eve precedes All Saints Day, the celebration of saints. A magician is by no stretch of the imagination a saint. He is more commonly considered a deceiver. But actually, Eric, I found this outfit in a storage room of theatrical costumes. It might be Halloween, for all I know, but I've lost all track of the calendar. It might as easily be Easter or your birthday, who knows? Regardless, I set out to celebrate my faith in magic by dressing the part. I suppose I would have been as pleased with a Wizard's smock with a cone-shaped cap of stars and moons, but the tux fit me perfectly, and I couldn't resist showing it off."

"You look very dapper. My name is Hattie," and she's already donned her brow swooping red hat for the occasion of introduction.

"Why thank you, young lady. You're looking quite snazzy yourself. What a pleasure to make your acquaintance." At this, Old Man Xavier extends a white gloved hand. He's wearing glassy black shiny shoes, and he takes care not to step on Hattie's bare toes, painted red. Of the rest of us, only Eric has his tennis shoes on. Zorra sits with her bare feet to one side on the couch, and I'm still lying on my side on my couch, my stocking feet against the armrest. Amelia appears to be deep asleep. She actually looks dead, the way she is posed like a soldier at attention, as if she were in a coffin. Fortunately I can make out the faint swelling and dropping of her chest.

Old Man Xavier's long gray beard covers his chest. If he's wearing a bow tie we never see it. He steps toward Amelia's couch, "I don't believe I know this renowned Mademoiselle."

Amelia stirs slightly, snorts, and then her eyelids lift. Hysteria set in, her arms covering her face, accompanied with a series of high pitched whinnies. Old Man Xavier steps back from the couch, and Hattie takes hold of Amelia's trembling hands, "It's OK, dear. Amelia, calm down, it's only a new friend of ours."

I fetch another cup of water for the poor, nerve-rattled gal. Hattie props Amelia up and pours a few sips of water over her dry lips. Poor Amelia's hair looks like a crashed bird's nest. "Lordy, lordy," she says. "I thought the Grim Reaper had come to take me."

"My apologies, madam. I was curious about such a worldly looking woman. Please forgive me if I have given you a fright. My name is Xavier."

"Not at all. You are quite a gentleman. I must say that I am not accustomed to meeting strangers upon awakening. Oh, dear, I must look a mess."

Hattie takes Amelia to the restroom in the hallway to freshen up while Old Man Xavier sits with Zorra and Eric. I put on my shoes and go to the men's room myself. By the time I return, Old Man Xavier decides that after breakfast we all need to make a visit to the Herbalist. He points out that Zorra has been despondent and bedridden for far too long, and our newcomer, Amelia, has turned into a nervous wreck.

In the cafeteria, I can imagine hidden cameras in the overhead neon fixtures. The view is of the tops of our heads, and our breakfast selections are arranged before us. Old Man Xavier and I are the only coffee drinkers. Zorra drinks orange juice while the older women have hot tea. Eric downs at least three little cartons of milk, along with lasagna and fried chicken. Zorra has selected scrambled eggs and sausages, while the rest of us eat cold cereal and oatmeal. The cafeteria has the atmosphere of an institution, giving me that trapped feeling of being back in school and that worn out feeling of taking a break at work.

The door to the Herbalist's shop is black-pepper brown. Old Man Xavier holds the door open for the ladies. I trail in last behind Zorra and Eric. I had expected the Herbalist to be old, perhaps Chinese, but this is a young man with an elegant black goatee and a turquoise turban. There is a jewel on the front of the turban shaped like a candle flame. The jewel seems to be a coral pink opal. The Herbalist may be Islamic or Hindu. He is exceptionally handsome,

The Herbalist looks up from his consultation with a client. He is describing something to a short woman in a peach colored shawl, draped over the back of her head. His eyes seem to be lined in theatrical black paint, like a silent movie star. His large, black, gleaming eyes take us in, not defensively, but with astuteness. A glass counter separates the Herbalist from the tiny woman being consulted. Inside the glass casing, there are tall slender jars with lizards suspended in fluids, jars filled with what looks like colored sand, and others that contain shriveled leaves and striped seeds. One wide jar houses small intestines coiled tightly within, if not the raveling gray pattern of brains. In a small pumpkin shaped jar, is a rosy gel with suspended bubbles and a halved egg, exposing the preserved embryo of a pink and featherless bird.

Eric whispers into my ear, "I thought that herbs were made of plants only."

"Apparently this guy is prepared for a diverse assortment of cures," I whisper back.

Behind the Herbalist stretches a long wall of tiny wooden drawers in perfect grid pattern. Each drawer is labeled with squiggles and spidery insignias that could be Sanskrit, Arabic, Hebrew, or Chinese for all I know. The Herbalist is writing on a long slip of yellow paper. I notice that the opal on his turban has turned ice blue. He places his hand over the head of the short woman and gazes into her eyes. I cannot see the woman's face, but the Herbalist shifts his gaze from one of her eyes to the other. He takes his hand off the woman's head, turns toward the array of tiny wooden drawers, raises a finger above his turban, and moves down the row toward the desired drawer. I observe him gently pulling out an extremely long drawer. He extracts a snarled black root. Then again, it might be a dried snake, I'm not sure. He slides the black thing into a narrow envelope and scribbles a few notes on the envelope's lip before sealing it and sliding it toward the small woman. The woman is patting the counter with her wrinkled hand, and I hear her squawking voice. I don't recognize the language. The words sound like a voice played backwards on a tape recording. The Herbalist is nodding and the little woman picks up the yellow slip of paper and envelope, drops them into a shoulder pouch, and turns to leave. Only a sliver of her face is visible from beneath the peach colored hood, and the sagging flesh is as creased as a dried apple.

Old Man Xavier takes Amelia's hand and steps up to the counter. Zorra takes a seat. Her chair is intricately carved teak. Behind her is the reflection of the chair's back in the wall mirror. The narrow shop is duplicated by this mirror, which serves to visually relieve the cramped feeling of this closely constructed room. The mirror also serves to assist the Herbalist in keeping an eye, front and back, on his clients. In the mirror I see that we make a diverse and colorful clientele. I also notice that Amelia's skin looks blacked out, as if she were wearing a black leotard over her face and hands. I turn away from the mirror, and her hands look pale and creamy pink. Her face and neck may be heavily coated with makeup, but the color is very light and fair. I turn again to the mirror and the rest of us are unaltered by the reflection. Hattie's skin is a very dark shade of brown, but even her reflection looks natural. Only Amelia, where her flesh is visible, is blackened out. The mirror is canceling her out.

CURE ALLS

We transform the cafeteria into a science lab, each of us with our own individually prescribed "herbal" cure from the Herbalist. Amelia's ailment went beyond a bad case of jangled nerves. The Herbalist described her condition as phantom syndrome, a condition he considered rare among the living. If a person crosses over into the realms of death and manages, for some unexplained reason, to return to life, he might easily be susceptible to phantom syndrome, a jittery and overwhelming inability to trust the realm of living spirits, along with haunting recollections of the death experience. Hot flashes, white-outs, blackouts, sweats, fainting, along with extreme irritability and nervousness are typical symptoms. Amelia's treatment was a combination therapy. At the Herbalist's shop, she was given a tranquilizing tea (a mixture or roots, berries, and leaves). The tea was bitter, but Amelia drank it all down without complaint.

Zorra was diagnosed next, while Amelia dozed off, with her head tilted back, seated in the high-backed teak chair. The Herbalist explained to Zorra that the potion he would prepare next was also for Amelia. It was considered preferable that the client suffering from phantom syndrome be unaware of the ingredients of the second potion, which included the juices of the baby bird embryo, powdered heart membrane, royal bee jelly, and the crushed wings of horse flies. A body that has experienced death requires a potion of living tissue to remind itself of the nature of being alive. The mixture formed a waxy ball of dough that could be melted and mixed with warm milk. "Add some chocolate syrup to cover up the ugly color," the Herbalist suggested.

Zorra's condition, though serious, was easily treatable. Her depression was an advanced progression of a common sleep disorder. All of the ingredients of her new sleep medication were simple powders made from roots and flower blossoms. The only animal ingredient was a trace extract of snake venom taken from a snake that could harm, but not kill you. The venom, in small dosage, served as a stimulant that triggered the healthy functioning of glands, hormones, and circulation. "Sleep deprivation can be very exhausting and depressing. Advanced cases of sleep deprived subjects can, as a result of exhaustion, become bedridden and are frequently mistaken as lazy, sleep addicted, good-for-nothing bums." The Herbalist smiled at Eric, who was eaves dropping on Zorra's consultation.

Old Man Xavier was given a mixture of longevity-aphrodisiac rejuvenating potion, and the bearded magician clicked his heels three times upon being handed his envelope. Hattie was given a vitamin enforced tree bark tea as a treatment for allergies to cats. Eric was encouraged to eat more vegetables, and the Herbalist slipped him a small package of green tea with tiny red berries "known to improve your masculine magnetism." The Herbalist gave me a wink when Eric took the package.

The Herbalist said that I was prone to worry and suffered mild cases of nervous tension. The herbs he suggested were a combination of mild stimulant and low grade sedative, combined with a subdued spider venom similar to Zorra's trace extract of snake venom. "Just to give the ol' organs a good kick start," said the Herbalist, as if he were a hick doc from the Midwest. The spider venom came in a salve to be applied behind the ears like perfume. Unfortunately, it smelled like cat piss and burned the skin slightly.

Zorra manages to heat some milk for Amelia, secretly dissolving the wax ball of living tissue, and stirring in a lavish amount of thick chocolate syrup. "The Herbalist recommended that you follow up your nerve tea with some nice hot chocolate to coat your stomach and prevent nausea." Amelia is dreamy-eyed and feeling no pain as she accepted the hot cocoa graciously. Zorra not only makes an excellent nurse, she has a gift for being sly.

THE SPIRITS GATHER

Old Man Xavier wheels an ornate and monstrous calliope into the couch room and has invited an open house of guests to the couch room. Zorra is already familiar with the remote control panels hidden in the couch arms. Xavier wears his top hat and tails while he performs a delicate overture of his own compositions. On the calliope, with its steam whistles and merry-go-round atmosphere, the music ranges from comical and high-spirited to sentimental, mysterious, and unnervingly suspenseful. Wall panels slide automatically as the dim light in the room grows darker still. A large blue screen appears from behind the panels. Voila, we are in a movie theater. The only missing ingredients are the popcorn and soda drinks.

The actors and action of the screen presentation are various housemates here in the House of Mind Games. The "film," if it is indeed a film, is frequently time-lapsed photography, giving the actors that nervous, highly animated fast pace of the silent movie era of the turn of the century and nineteen twenties. Early shots include Old Man Xavier back before anyone would have thought to call him old. Xavier sports a dark and well trimmed goatee and a full head of slicked back hair. He is not yet noticeably wrinkled and his physic and facial features are far less affected by the years of gravitationally induced sag. He actually looks dashing and invigorated. He is seen riding a bicycle through the old fashioned hallway. He passes undamaged through walls and furniture, and is even seen bicycling among the clouds in the sky, passing by colored doors that float among the clouds. I see that he has taken on the challenge that I had turned away from. (It also crosses my mind that I encountered this sky full of doors in the contemporary hallway, not the old corridor. I'll have to ask Xavier about this later.)

Another scene stars two attractive women draped in diaphanous robes roaming a woods of aspen trees. The wind playfully vibrates and twirls the coin shaped leaves of the aspens, and the women appear and disappear at random among the white tree trunks. A visual game of hide and seek and seek and hide is innocently accompanied by Xavier's playful and ethereal modulations on the calliope. A foreboding flock of gargantuan ravens swoop down from the sky. With their reptilian talons clasping the powder white arms of the two women, the ravens ascend, their massive black wings languidly rising and falling. The women soar gracefully skyward, posed like angels, and yet with an air of terror amid the flock of dark wings, stealing them away. I recall the same horror, watching winged monkeys snatch Dorothy and the Lion and the Scarecrow from the dark forest of the witch's castle.

There are close-ups of the women's faces, matured cupids. Their porcelain white complexions form the sculpted canvases for long shadows that slide up and down their serene gazes. I realize suddenly that these women are Mimi and the old woman with the red dress, white hair and pearls. They were so stunning when they were young.

The next scene is comical, and Xavier accentuates the frantic rhythm of the time-lapsed segment. It involves Eric, Zorra, and me, camping out in the apartment, watching the old Zenith television. The camera shot is from the Zenith television (which explains the occasional sensations I had of being watched). The three of us lean forward, glued to the news, and then one of us whisk away in a blur and reappear in a snap with drinks and snacks that we devour frantically and neurotically. The disappearance of food and drinks occurs so rapidly, we appear to consume like powerful vacuum cleaners. I disappear briefly, during which Eric makes quick awkward gestures of romance that are readily spurned by Zorra. When I reappear, they both resume more innocent poses. There are a series of musical chair flurries and blurred activities in which all three of us scamper left and right before the camera like panicked birds in a cage. Then, bam, we all sit glued to the news again like hypnotized zombies.

The entire segment only lasts four or five minutes. The audience laughs and howls. I'm reasonably sure that both Eric and Zorra feel a similar embarrassment to my own. We had no idea we were being recorded, and I feel a heat rise to my face that is a combination of aggravation and shame at the loss of personal privacy. Smile! You're on candid camera.

The final segment is probably my favorite. Xavier's calliope composition verges upon classical and ecclesiastic rapture as a series of people dive into the swimming pool, transformed into an underwater metamorphosis of altered self; a moth, a dragonfly, a snowy owl, a quetzal, a leopard, a swallow, a caribou, a mustang , and a greyhound. I find myself truly mesmerized by the graceful drifting of underwater choreography.

The lights go up and there is a standing ovation. The mingling of voices and shuffling of feet recreate a long lost experience of a congenial crowd, chattering amongst each other and clamoring to congratulate Old Man Xavier on his score. We are as bubbly as a cocktail party, and temporarily (I think) everyone in the crowd develops a brief case of amnesia. We forget that we were real people who have lost contact with reality.

LATE NIGHT THOUGHTS

The chatter and merriment of the crowd carry out into the hallway. The slender, elongated stained-glass V lamps shine like searchlights amid the mingling residents. Several of us meander to the cafeteria for snacks. I pop some corn and pour some diet soda over ice, a craving brought on by the atmosphere of a movie theater. We come to call the night Home Movies. They are films of us.

I eventually return to the couch room to stretch out on a couch and find Amelia, Zorra, and Eric already settling in. Zorra informs me that Hattie has gone back to the tan door, and by making a U turn in the entryways of shelved heads, she ha returned to check on her mobile home park. Eric has accompanied her, to make sure she didn't get lost. Apparently, the brush fires had not reached the mobile homes, and her trailer was untouched. We had all stored her collection of hats on several of the catalogued heads, so Eric helps her to gather the hats and reinstall them in their fiberglass cases on her living room walls.

"Home, sweet, home," Hattie says, when the last hat was placed back on display. Eric does not really have a personal context for such a feeling as *home-sweet-home,* but he pats her on the shoulder and smiles before bidding her good night. He can see why Hattie would like the simple refuge of such a personalized home.

I wake from a disturbing dream, unable to recall what it had been about. I step out into the quiet hallway and head for the restroom to relieve myself. Returning from the restroom to the couch room, I hear a far off wailing as I cross the hallway. I stop to listen. The voice is female, and the sound echoes. It's laughter. A far off laughter that echoes in the hallway, the laughter seems to be unending. I remember entering the foyer with the odd little man, my first day here. He had looked up at a defunct laughing lady, a mechanical automaton that was out of order. I remember him saying that sometimes he heard her laughter, like a far off ghost from the past. When he said it,

I had thought that he sounded a little off in the head. He was telling me that he heard voices and I thought it sounded corny.

Now I hear the lady laughing, and it doesn't sound corny. It sounds sad. It sounds lonely. A desperate laugh is not a joyful laugh. I cover my ears and head back to the couch room. Everything is quiet inside. I lie on the couch and think about the odd little guy who let me in. He had his own room just inside the first door with the mirror. He had a sign on the door that read DO NOT DISTURB. Why on earth have I remained so logical? In such an illogical place as this, there is no real sense in complying with a sign that reads DO NOT DISTURB. Tomorrow, when Eric wakes up, I'm going to run this by him. We should march right back to that door and knock. Hopefully, the renovation of the old hallway will be complete. We haven't been back there for a while now. I never stepped all the way through that mirror, either. The odd little doorman had also said that there was no way out of here. If I throw all logic to the wind, I have no need to trust his statement. There must be a way out of here. I feel it in my bones. There's a way out. There has to be.

AMELIA'S ABNORMAL BEHAVIOR

Zorra is up early and looking more chipper than we've seen her in a long time. She has her hair up in a French roll, and she is even wearing shoes. Eric is pleased to see her improvement. He proposes that they spend a day of "exploring." Zorra seems pleased with the idea.

Old Man Xavier had slipped off after the Home Movie, and Hattie is back at home in her trailer. I sit up feeling groggy. I place my stocking feet on the floor and listen to Eric planning an eventful day with Zorra. I need my morning coffee, but I do remember that I want to suggest to Eric that we knock on the odd little guy's door marked DO NOT DISTURB.

Amelia is still asleep. She is mumbling in her sleep, tossing and turning. Occasionally she twitches, or her arms and legs jerk. Maybe she is having a dream about the electric chair. I decide to spring my idea on Eric before my first cup of coffee. It looks as though they'll be departing before I can pull my shoes on. He suggests that since he has committed his day to Zorra, I might want to check the glass doors today to see if they are still locked. It sounds like a good idea.

Eric and Zorra are just about out the door, and wishing me a good day, when Amelia wakes up screaming. Zorra takes a few steps in Amelia's direction, but halts abruptly when a huge burst of flame consumes the couch where Amelia lies. As suddenly as the flame has ignited, it's gone, but there on the couch, where Amelia had been, Mimi sits, hunched over with one golden eye open. The look in that eye is as cold as a lizard. Mimi sees the three of us. We all freeze like victims of a stun gun. The huge flame reappears with a loud whoosh of air. We all feel the igniting flame like a strong burst of hot desert wind in our faces. Instantaneously, the flame vanishes. Like a flash-in-the-pan magician's trick, Amelia is gone, along with Mimi, and the only remnant is a dark ring of black smoke in the room and the charred, steaming couch.

"Not again," says Eric.

"Am I crazy or did I see Mimi sitting on that couch?" asks Zorra.

"It was Mimi alright. I don't know if she came back, or Amelia turned into Mimi. I'm not sure what just happened!" I admit, shaking my head.

"Does this mean we're getting another puppet-show funeral in Amelia's honor?"

We all gaze at the blacken couch, still giving off smoke. "It beats me. It looks like we have shrine number two."

"Who is going to burst into flame next?" asked Zorra, with exasperation.

"Let's get out of here," Eric proposed.

"I think you're right, Eric. Do you think we should throw some water on the couch? I wondered. "If the couch's stuffing reignited, the whole place could burn down."

Eric and Zorra leave for their outing. I bring back a couple of cups of water from the cafeteria to soak the singed couch. It looks like the smoke has died out, but the whole room now smells like burned rope. I would open a window, but the room had no windows. I grab a few bites of oatmeal in the cafeteria and down some coffee before heading down the hall to check on the progress of the renovation and the locked glass doors.

The glass doors were still locked, but the old hallway has been cleared of the white canvases. This is a promising sign of progress. Here I am again, alone in the hallway. I saunter down the hallway, taking in the variation of door colors. I notice a large terra cotta colored door that I hadn't tried yet. Am I ready for some huge traumatic experience? On the other hand, am I ready for an enchanted escapade? I never know which way the experience would go. Sometimes one experience goes both ways. I definitely have grown tired of the cafeteria, and now the couch room is haunted. Here I go.

I turned the brass knob on the terra cotta door, and pushed it open. (I still have my ring of skeleton keys for the old hallway, but keys are not needed here.) The floor is hardwood. I open the door wider and see a hardwood floor that disappears under a forest green carpet. The room looks like a library or a bookstore. I step into the room, letting the door close behind me. I don't notice another soul in the place, only rows of shelves with hundreds of book. This gives me a wonderful feeling. I love libraries and bookstores. Each book is an involved message from a living, breathing human being. These messages, these views into the conscience and consciousness of others, are left behind for us to discover. It is both exciting and a little daunting. There are so many stories and subjects that don't appeal to me. Sometimes I feel like I'm looking for a needle in a haystack when I look through shelves of books. I have learned a little trick that helps me select a captivating text. I stop and close my eyes and say a quick prayer, "God, please guide me to discover a magical book that I will enjoy and appreciate. Please, God, help me select a book that will stir my emotions and ignite my interest and sense of intrigue. Please help to catch my eye with the book you would have me read."

I say this prayer and then open my eyes. I look at titles and colors. Some books have cover artwork that catches my eye. I walk down one aisle and turn down the next. I pull out an oversized book with an intricately embossed border and the cover illustration of a fire breathing dragon. Fire breathing dragons make good fairytales, but I've seen better here in the House of Mind Games. I put the book back and take a few more steps, watching the bindings scroll past my shoulder. I pull out a book called *The Mastermind*. The story looks a little too science fiction for my taste. I put it back. A dried-mustard colored book with light-blue lettering stands out from a higher shelf. The title is The Amusement Park. Either it's an ironic prank, or coincidentally happens to be a suspense novel that I would normally pass up. I pull the clay-mustard colored book from the shelf and open to the first page:

You shouldn't have come here, but you did. You couldn't have resisted. It may seem like you didn't choose this book any more than you choose to be here. Opinions clash concerning the theory that existence is a choice. Existence may feel more precisely as if it were put upon us. "I was sent here," you might say. I'm not even going to tell you to go back where you just came from. The "other self," the "subterranean self," the "subconscious, or dreamed self" are all part of existence. You are bound to make visits to these altered dimensions of your own self, without my encouragement. Here you are, in a world of logic and rules. There are competitions for wealth, security, looks and recognition. There are a variety of acceptable etiquettes, displays of rebellion, and there is work, work, and more work. There are endless choices of food, clothing, shopping, movies, and theaters. We discover books and friends and family and love and hate and war and lots of traffic. Pleasure is too slippery to nail down, and suffering insists on barging in, uninvited. There are good books and strange dreams and there is a wonderful sense of accomplishment of a job well done, and moments of wonder and also of despair. It's all very complicated, unless, of course, you decide to keep things simple. "How does one simplify his life?" you might ask.

I shut the book and place it, face down, on my blue bedspread. Here I am, in my very own bed, in my rented apartment. I get up, check the clock and the calendar, and say hello to my roommate. I learn that I still have my job, and I didn't even miss paying the rent. My roommate says I was merely reading, nothing unusual. What I don't know yet, but I am bound to find out, is that there is another book hidden under my bed. When I find the other book hidden under the bed, I will think twice before opening it. I will hide it again, but I will have no inclination of throwing it away. The book hidden under my bed is *The Unamusement Park*.

Walter Black was born in Kansas, his mother's name was Dorothy, but she didn't have a little dog named Toto. He did, however, get blown over the rainbow and landed in California. He composed and performed film music and pop songs in San Francisco, and then migrated south to San Diego, where he painted and sold his own art. He is the author of three novels;

The Unamusement Park,

Captivating the Escape Artist,

and The Jeweler's Apprentice.

available at Lulu.com

The Amusement Park is a theater-of-the-absurd tale of Jacob, a delivery driver for a mattress store. After being warned to not enter, Jacob finds himself lost inside an infinite hallway of multicolored doors. Like Aldous Huxley's DOORS OF PERCEPTION, the doors lead to new realms of Jacob's mind and imagination. As if trapped in a dream, Jacob first seek escape from the nightmarish hallway, but discoveries lead him to question his desire to return to his previous reality and the world he left behind.